SUN

for
JIMMY and the BEE!
Yen Ooi
APR 2016.

Sun

Queens of Earth

by Yen Ooi

This novel is a work of fiction. Any references to real people, events, establishments, organizations, or locales are intended only to give the fiction a sense of reality and authenticity, and are used fictitiously. All other names, characters, and places, and all dialogue and incidents portrayed in this book are the product of the author's imagination.

Sun: Queens of the Earth

For information address:

Spectacle Publishing Media Group

P.O. Box 295,

Lisle, NY 13797

First Spectacle Paperback Published 2014

Cover design by Jake Giddens and Eric Staggs
Interior design by Whitney Smyth
Author Photo by Kenneth Loh

ISBN 978-1-938444-09-8

For Kenneth, who didn't try to wake sleeping beauty,
instead he joined her in dreaming

Table of Contents

prologue

When I was born, humanity was blessed with two planets and a satellite that we called home, an abundance of resources and a rich history that we thought would provide us with enough intelligence and experience to deal with whatever life threw at us. What we did not realise was that it was just the beginning of another epoch in our Solar System. We dreamt of better technology, of starfaring capabilities, of first contact, but we never believed ourselves to be anything but superior. We never understood anything other than the selfish urges of being human—not even understanding humanity as a whole.

My parents, Horace and Magdalena, worked on Moon, on Near Side, where they had also conceived me. Wanting to provide me with the best they could, they placed me in the best care affordable. I was moved to the nearby planet, Kagami, and they went to Earth where they spent the rest of their lives working with Coughin machines. I never really knew them save for the letters they sent as I was growing up, which I am very grateful for. I realise now that it was more than many of my friends had in a world that was starting to crumble under its own weight.

I live on Earth now with my best friend, the love of my life, my partner, Maaike. Humanity has shrunken to occupy only this planet again, with Moon abandoned and Kagami out of our reach; a regression of sorts. There is much chaos around here, but Maaike and I are surprisingly calm. Even though our children are beyond our reach now, we have faith that the future will be a better place than what we know. A faith that people had previously placed in the trust of religion and God, we now place in ourselves, in humanity.

My name is Sun.

Kagami

chapter 1

At the main boardroom in Blue Planet's headquarters, the Royal Committee meeting took a turn and heated discussions could be heard. The glass walls, framing a view above clouds, did not seem to have any effect on the people. They were deep in conversation.

"This is the most important discovery for Blue Planet since we ended the Great War," Queen Catherine could be heard to say in the background, but before she could finish her sentence, she was interrupted by a louder, male voice.

"War, war, war! That's all you ever talk about. We have managed peace for twenty-two years now and you still dredge up the past on every occasion. Doesn't it bore you? This is a great *positive* discovery," King Johannes had spat out the word 'positive' to make his point.

Before anyone could respond, the Secretary, King Mumbaza, stood up and announced that the Board of Directors was waiting outside.

The Royal Committee moved with a sense of habit into their seats, their PAs standing directly behind them providing more administrative assistance than security. As soon as the shuffling stopped, King Mumbaza nodded to his assistant who was standing by the door to allow the Board of Directors to enter.

Representing the Chairs of the largest firms before the privatisation of Earth into Blue Planet Inc., each Board member entered with an air of caution, still uncomfortable with the lack of protocol in greeting the Royals.

"If we are all ready, I shall proceed," suggested King Mumbaza as a wave of nods rippled across the boardroom.

"You are all aware that we are here to discuss a discovery that was confirmed by scientists in Okinawa approximately eighteen hours ago, yes?"

Again, there were nods from all in attendance. King Mumbaza paused with a drink of water.

"The object of this discovery has been kept a secret so far in order to control the publicity on the matter. This is because the Royal Committee has not yet been able to come to a decision on how the discovery is to be handled. Discussions and ideas have been many, but agreements on the matter were few."

Expecting excitement to break out, King Mumbaza held his professional demeanour as he was greeted by a deeper silence instead.

"We have validated information that there is another planet within our solar system, one which we did not have prior knowledge of."

Most hands in the room were raised as the murmurs echoed in the boardroom. King Mumbaza hushed the room with a wave of his hand.

"We will have a session for questions after, so please note your concerns and enquiries for later." After a deep breath, he continued, "The new planet seems to mimic all of Earth's traits; atmosphere, water, gases, mountains, lakes, valleys. Actually, other than the topography, the layout of the lands and seas, it seems identical to Earth. From current data, there do not seem to be any signs of intelligent life forms on the planet, with just a basic array of flora and fauna when compared to Earth." In fact, Blue Planet scientists had been manically scouring the new planet through a variety of technology since its initial discovery a few months back. They knew that a revelation of this size would demand that the data presented be irreproachable.

Though difficult to believe, the planet, at every point of scrutiny, seemed to be in a state that was perfect for human possession, with very few natural threats.

Holding his hands up in preparation for an assault of questions, he was greeted by the eerie silence again.

"Scientists are still exploring how far the similarities go, but the resemblance so far has earned the planet its name, 'Kagamiboshi'. Our Okinawa colleagues had thought on discovery that Kagami was a reflection of Earth itself, an optical illusion of sorts."

"The only explanation that we have received from all the top scientists who are privy to this information as to why this planet was not discovered earlier was that it previously shared Earth's orbit, and circled the sun on the opposite side of the circuit. It would seem that Kagami was hiding in plain sight."

Now, life seemed to have returned to the boardroom as laughter and giggles can be heard.

"Unfortunately, that is not a joke. The hypothesis is that Kagami was recently knocked off its orbit, which was fully hidden from our detection, into plain view. If Kagami's orbit is stable now, scientists have calculated that we will be able to see it with just an ordinary telescope during the next full solar eclipse."

"Ladies and gents, the Royal Committee have made only one decision at the moment and we ask for your full support on this decision to help manage the reactions from civilians after the news goes out. We, the Royal Committee, have decided to keep Kagami preserved in its current state, barring anyone, scientist, military or civilian, from travelling to or landing on the planet until further notice. Science exploration will be kept to robotic probes only."

This led to a full uproar from the Board of Directors, everyone with their own concerns and questions, whilst the Royal

Committee stared on, aware that their own tumult earlier was the same. Queen Catherine brought her palms up to her head, massaging her temples as the din started to encourage a migraine. Prince Mohamed sat back in his chair and smiled nonchalantly. They all knew the impossibility of the situation.

King Mumbaza failed to quiet the crowd and reached for the button directly in front of him. His touch triggered an alarm that brought the crowd to a natural silence again.

"The reason for the preservation of Kagami is to ensure that the planet and any resources that it may hold will be treated fairly and with respect. Ladies and gents, you can surely understand the need for preservation after the countless meetings we have had together on the problems we are facing with the Earth's ecosystem. Whatever ideology you may hold or reject, believe that we have been given a second chance; a perfect planet to be treated with respect, considering all the past mistakes that have been made."

"Banning manned explorations of Kagami is not a long-term plan. This will be a temporary arrangement whilst we open up the opportunity to tender to you. Yes, you, the Board of Directors."

"The Royal Committee has been at a loss on how to proceed and so, in practicing the corporate democracy of Blue Planet, we open up the opportunity to you, to send in applications for tender for the future of Kagami. Each firm represented on this Board can only present one proposal to the Royal Committee. We have set out some general parameters for this and set a deadline for three years from today, so please take your time to consider how you will approach this, and before we proceed further, we invite you all to break for lunch first. You know your way to the dining area. Information packs are available to be downloaded at lunch. We will convene for your questions in exactly one hour from now. Thank you."

The Board of Directors dispersed from the boardroom more quickly than they had entered it. They were all deep in conversations with their accompanying representatives, some glad to have brought along their head of strategy or CEO, others coping with the PR and marketing suggestions of their Communications Head.

As the last Director left the room, the Royal Committee members breathed a sigh of relief. Queen Silvia was the first to stand, heading straight for the door.

"Well," she said. "It has begun. I will finalise the preparations for the virtual press conference. Mumbaza," she turned to address the Secretary, "if I receive no news from you during the Q&A, we will proceed as planned."

King Mumbaza nodded in affirmation to Queen Silvia as she walked out of the door with Ronaldo, her assistant, trailing behind, both with the same sway.

They all knew that the scientists were busy scanning Kagami for as much information as possible and that work will not slow down, not until there was a solution to what they were going to do with Kagami.

"What a drama queen," whispered King Johannes as soon as Queen Silvia was out of earshot. Although Queen Silvia was seen as the bitch of the Committee, they had chosen her to head up Blue Planet's communications precisely because she was very good at her job. No doubt her team would be tested to their limits with the information about Kagami. As soon as the first press release was made, not long after King Mumbaza concluded the briefing session with the Board of Directors, citizens would be kept abreast with all the developments and findings of Kagami. Nothing would be kept from the public eye from then onwards.

"This is not the time to joke, Johannes," snarled Queen Catherine, with her palms still holding her temples.

"Yes indeed, you are right Catherine. This is not the time to joke," he teased, "but to celebrate! Come on, blue bloods, can't you all see that this is a blessing? It's a gift. No one has died, and actually, this probably means that quality of life for all of humanity will be dramatically improved!"

Kaiser Mikhail got up and walked to the centre of the group, acknowledging everyone. "Johannes is right, you know. We should be grateful for this gift. Perhaps a prayer is in order. Anyway, when Blue Planet was created, the people insisted on the arrangement we have now and it is precisely for situations like this. So, we have to shirk our royal-ness and treat this as just another item on the agenda. We no longer have authority or responsibility over our people. They have the responsibility and authority now and we are just the puppets, doing their bidding. So, I shall be at the temple if anyone would like to join me."

One who had recently found solace in spirituality, Kaiser Mikhail used his newfound faith to help him reconnect with humanity, with citizens. Like many of the Royal Committee members, they struggled with the concept that their status as royalty meant nothing anymore and that that they were as dispensable as the next person. This was proven by the dismissal of Sultan Ibrahim by vote of citizens. Ibrahim had insisted that the work of a Royal, even in this new system, was still more than any other citizen's given that they would be expected to make difficult decisions involving the welfare of the people. This quickly backfired as not only was Ibrahim let go from his position, the citizens were quick to ensure that the constitution clearly stated that the Royal Committee was not to make any decisions affecting the nation. They could manage information to a certain extent and put out suggestions or choices of actions, but ultimately, decisions were all voted on by citizens. The process varied, as depending on the issue, voting could take place globally or state-wise, or even just within a community.

Of course, the Royal Committee members were still able to influence public decisions, but this became more difficult when equal portions of citizens respected and doubted the abilities of the Royal Committee members.

Although the meeting had been over for a while, the rest of the Royal Committee remained comfortable in their seats, each trying to decide on their next steps. This nearly never happened since all the Royals, like most citizens, were prepared to put in only the time needed for any given task, clocking only the required hours.

"Any additional words of advice before I head to the Q&A?" asked King Mumbaza, reluctantly getting up from his seat. His movements gave away his overweight past, contradicting his new athletic frame that was shrouded in a combination of simple linen shirt and trousers.

Queen Catherine looked up to King Mumbaza and smiled reassuringly. "You'll be fine, Mumbaza. We'll see you next week, when I'm sure we'll have much more to talk about."

Mumbaza looked back and smiled gratefully at Catherine before turning his heel to the crowd.

The Royal Committee dispersed with a mixture of emotions, each with a different veil. They were all used to hiding what they really felt. What they did not know was that every one of them was feeling the same thing at that moment, a raw piece of fear, gnawing in their gut, scared that what seemed to be a blessing might turn out to be a nightmare.

chapter 2

The darkness of the office, with only a soft glow coming from the display panel of the telephone, reminded everyone at Queen Catherine's office that she was experiencing yet another migraine. Her office was the only space dressed with antiques, mostly from the Victorian period, juxtaposed against the entire building made of glass and steel and the clean lines of Japanese furniture.

Queen Catherine was on the telephone, the latest model that had not even reached the shelves yet. Sleek, efficient, and with enough processing power to pilot an aircraft, it was the only other thing besides her tablet that was from the twenty-first century. It was a gift from Brend Zoid, chairman of Cyberity, who was on the other end of the telephone. Cyberity was Earth's biggest cyber security firm from before Blue Planet.

"Brend, thank you for consulting me at this point, but as I told you before, the Royals have relinquished all our power on this matter now."

"I understand, Cate, and I'm sorry to bother you during another migraine attack, but I just need to know if the Royals will have final say in judging the applications in 2064?"

"No, Brend," Queen Catherine sighed as she took a long sip of water. "Judging will be by the people and that is the only thing I am allowed to say at this point. I can assure you that not a single one of us will be able to determine the outcome. It will be as fair as the people insisted twenty-two years ago."

With both parties exasperated, Brend accepted defeat and changed his tone. "Ok. Let me put some things in order here and I'll come by and pick you up, Cate. You need to see Dahl about that migraine of yours."

Knowing that Brend would insist until she gave in, Catherine grunted in agreement and hung up the telephone. Dr. Freya Dahl, unknown to most in the medical field, was the best experimental migraine specialist around. A close friend of Brend's, Queen Catherine had her own ideas about the type of relationship Brend and Dahl had before. But as the trend is to forget the past, something that Cate was unable to do, she tried to accept Brend's friendship for what it was and counted her blessings that the practice of espionage was more or less over.

Brend arrived at Queen Catherine's office an hour later as Catherine and her PA, Sarah, tidied up her office for the day. They took the service elevator situated just behind her office as they do every day.

As they arrived at the private vehicles area, Sarah moved forward to do initial checks, out of habit now rather than necessity, before opening the back door for Catherine. Sarah then took her place next to the driver, Charles, who was Brend's PA. The four took the journey with a sense of familiarity.

At Dr. Dahl's office, only Brend and Catherine entered the building, leaving Sarah and Charles waiting in the car. Dr. Dahl always cleared the clinic for their visits, so there would be no need for additional security. On that day, however, Queen Catherine and Brend were surprised to see that there was another man sitting in the waiting room of the clinic as they walked in.

"Cate, Brend, it's so good to see you," Dr. Dahl greeted them with an exaggerated warmth.

"Freya, you look great as always," replied Brend, adding in a whisper, "who's the other patient?"

With a gentle arm on Queen Catherine's shoulder, Freya told them that he was not a patient, but a colleague, and moved to introduce them.

"This is the brains behind my practice, Dr. Nemo Coughin. His ancestry is a little difficult to trace, but I have been assured that his surname, though spelt c-o-u-g-h-i-n, is to be pronounced Koog-hun. Nemo, this is my newest patient, Queen Catherine and my old friend Brend Zoid."

As hands were shaken, Queen Catherine, in obvious pain, addressed the situation. "Freya, I'm sorry to be rude, but it's really bad today and I don't think I am in any state to make new friends."

"I do apologise, Cate, for not explaining better. Nemo here has made a breakthrough in migraine science and we think that we have found what could be a method to manage your condition."

Queen Catherine managed a nod as she made her way through to the inner office of the clinic, Brend ushering her gently by the arm.

As they settled in Dr. Dahl's office, she moved to administer a shot of strong painkiller directly to the base of Queen Catherine's neck so that the relief would be immediate. Leaving Brend and Catherine to their own for a few minutes, Dr. Dahl handed a glass of water to Brend and nodded towards the door to the lab, suggesting that they make their way over when Queen Catherine had recovered.

It was only a few minutes later when Catherine and Brend joined Dr. Dahl and Dr. Coughin in the laboratory.

"Feeling better, Cate?"

"Yes, thanks."

"That should hopefully be the last time you will need Xcava or any other painkillers for your migraines. Let's show you the solution we have for you," Dr. Dahl pointed to two seats near the back of the room as Dr. Coughin set up a projection.

They watched the five-minute presentation in silence, as the 3D display graphically explained the surgical procedure, overlaid with a mechanical voice-over using long medical terms effortlessly. As the presentation completed, Dr. Dahl reached over to switch on the lights.

"Ok, so, you're planning to stick a microchip in my brain just at the base of my neck."

"That is a very crude summary of the presentation, but yes," Dr. Coughin responded with a throaty laugh.

"Now that I know what you want to do, can you explain why and how, without the medical jargon please?"

"Of course, Queen Catherine."

"If you're going to take my skull apart, I think you should call me Cate, Nemo." They smiled at each other, lightening the mood in the laboratory.

"In layman's terms, though you're anything but a layperson, Cate," he added with a sly grin, Dr. Coughin explained how they had isolated the main nerve that causes 99.2% of cases of migraines. Having worked with biological engineers for over ten years, Dr. Coughin discovered that a small computer chip could be attached to the nerve to create a by-pass that isolated the migraine to a small area that does not have any pain receptors.

"And how is this chip controlled?"

"Ah, that's where the genius comes in. The chip isn't controlled. It acts like a muscle, or like an electric circuit. The impulse of regular brain movements and the impulse of a migraine have been identified and isolated. When the migraine kicks in, the impulse is seen by the chip to be the wrong kind of impulse and so closes the gate, disallowing any flow. However, normal brain movements, normal thinking and reactions will be allowed through. So, the gates will open and close for the different impulses, ensuring that the migraine impulses will always be barred from going any further."

"That actually sounds simple. Is there a catch?" Queen Catherine said as she subconsciously reached out to Brend for reassurance.

"The catch is the same as any other surgery. There is a chance that the surgery will go wrong, that you react to anesthesia, that you might die from complications, that the chip doesn't work. The list goes on Cate, but to clarify, we won't need to break your skull apart. In fact, the whole thing can be done as key-hole surgery."

"Ok, ignoring all the normal surgical implications, what are the concerns for this specific surgery? What's the worst case scenario?"

"If wrongly managed, the chip might stop or impair all impulses into your brain. You would then be paralysed or brain-dead, for a while, but that is reversible by removing the chip. Otherwise, the chip could just not work, leaving you exactly as you are now."

"And what is the success rate for the procedure, as of today?"

"Eight attempts, a hundred percent success, but all on primates, not humans."

"I would be the first human to have this?"

"No, we have scheduled our first human patient surgery for tomorrow morning. The earliest we will be able to schedule you in would be in a week's time. At that point, we would have had three human patients before you."

"Ok. Slot me in for next week."

"Are you sure?" interjected Brend, who had been quietly absorbing the situation.

"Yes, Brend. I have the week to change my mind, during which I can study all the information closely. Until then, this all sounds too good to pass on."

"Brend, please don't worry," added Dr. Dahl. "I wouldn't have recommended that Cate do this unless I was sure that it is the best option. I will prepare two sets of materials on the full information of the procedure so that you may both study it. Brend, Cate, have your own scientists look at it if you're concerned. We don't mind at all and, if anything, it would be good publicity for us."

"Yes, and the choice will always be yours, Cate," added Dr. Coughin.

"As I said earlier, I think this is the right decision for now. Please book me in for next week and we will study the materials in the meantime. Any questions, we'll be in touch with Freya. Agreed?"

Dr. Dahl nodded as Catherine and Brend collected their things to leave the clinic.

Charles pulled the car up to meet Queen Catherine and Brend at the clinic entrance. Both Charles and Sarah were aware of a certain tension or excitement but remained professional and made no remark.

"Sir, where would you like to go now?" asked Charles as they pulled away from the clinic.

"Brend," interjected Queen Catherine, "I think we should head to our favourite restaurant for a celebratory dinner, if you aren't needed at the office, of course."

Brend nodded at Queen Catherine and said to Charles, "You heard the lady." Smiling, he caught Charles and Sarah throwing a questioning look at each other.

Chapter 3

Before we met, your *mother and I were from difficult backgrounds. My father–your grandfather Frank–suffered from Alzheimer's disease. The community looked down on us for it as we shunned care that the government offered. As long as it was still our choice, Grandmother Frank was adamant that your grandfather would stay with us, in our own care for as long as possible. This degenerative disease is treatable at most levels, but it had surpassed all treatable stages when we found out that Grandfather Frank had it. We knew as well that most patients who moved into a treatment centre did not last very long. There were rumours, but no one would come out and say it straight out. They all died of different causes, of different illnesses, but they all died quickly.*

Because of your grandfather's condition, your grandmother and I could only work partially, contributing to the community only as low-output citizens. The community pressured us to put Grandfather Frank in the treatment centres, so that we could increase our output, but we held on as much as we could. The offer from Virgin Red Bull to work on Moon came somewhat as a godsend, as it would mean that we could all work, increase our outputs and yet be able to care for your grandfather.

Your mother's story is somewhat more tragic. Her parents loved her dearly and worked extra shifts so that she didn't have to. As a family unit, they had a good output level, even though your mother never worked, but the community didn't care as long as the family unit was ok.

It was only a couple of months before we had decided to move to Moon when your mother's parents met with a freak transport accident that killed them both on the spot. She found herself alone and lost, without any working experiences to support herself. When she heard about the opportunity on Moon, she took it to avoid being questioned in her own community.

As Queen Catherine entered the Blue Planet boardroom, she saw Prince Mohamed standing in the middle, staring out of the glass windows that offered a view above the clouds. Dressed in a light brown summer suit, he looked like any other person off the streets. It was a fashion that promoted the anonymity that citizens wanted so badly after the Great War; an equal world where money held no value and jobs were only to sustain the community. Only activity credits held any form of value now, and even then, it was all appropriated by the amount of effort and time spent on a job. Being a Royal Committee member may bring more comforts in their surroundings and facilities, but that was the only upside to the job.

Queen Catherine followed Prince Mohamed's sight line, looking into the blue skies with only spires with aircraft warning lights visible at this height.

"Sometimes, I think perhaps this is the closest to heaven we will get," tried Queen Catherine, unsure of what mood Prince Mohamed might be in.

"Yes, that was in my thoughts. What if heaven is just this and when we die, we'll go someplace that is less beautiful?"

"Well, then I would say that beauty is a state of mind, so just come back to this memory and you'll find beauty."

"But that would suggest that we would need our memories in heaven, which I would rather not do with."

"Well, then, you won't remember that you have seen something more beautiful than heaven!"

They both laughed at the turn of their conversation, feeling sheepish, as if they were caught in a sinful act.

"What were you thinking of when I disturbed you earlier?"

"Oh, just that we used to celebrate the Sultan's birthday on the fifteenth of July, before Blue Planet."

"I remember the celebrations you had. I had only seen them on television, but they were always known as the biggest birthday parties in the world."

"Yes, and now, because we are equal with everyone else, we are allowed a cake, some candles and perhaps a glass of alcohol, if we weren't Muslim."

Feeling his melancholy, Queen Catherine asked quietly, "Is it your father's real birthday today?"

He nodded ever so slightly, and then added a soft laugh. "Regardless of who was Sultan, the fifteenth of July was always celebrated by our old nation as the Sultan's birthday. Now that it is actually the true birthday of the Sultan, it is not celebrated anymore. Would it be the correct use of the word 'irony' in this context?" he asked as he gazed at Queen Catherine, taking time to linger on her marble-like grey eyes.

Suddenly feeling exposed, she looked to her feet, aware that she was blushing from her breasts up. She just nodded, her striking black hair bounced in its hard bob cut. She would not trust herself to say anything more.

Conscious of her discomfort, Prince Mohamed changed the topic. "You look well, Catherine. I hear that you were cured of your migraines?"

Glad for the diversion, she dived into a long explanation of the procedure, adding in the end that, "There haven't been any side effects at all."

"A second chance, just like Kagami," Prince Mohamed whispered, barely audible as the room started filling up with a few more Royal members.

They took their positions and King Mumbaza opened the meeting, summarising the events of the month before. There were only two agenda points to be discussed, one about the issue of non-active civilians and the other about the progress of the tender applications for Kagami.

"The summary from all the state representatives is that non-active civilians are starting to be seen as pests amongst their communities. Now that we have managed to phase out all things monetary and introduce output based living incentives, low-output civilians are slowly being casted out. Even if they have the capacity and skills to compete and increase output, the community is creating non-formal barriers against them."

"Go on Catherine, say something about the past," teased King Johannes.

"Just because you taunt me about it Johannes, it won't stop me from voicing my opinion. This is the same behaviour that was provoked by the class systems in a capitalist environment. It's unfortunately what it is to be human and to compete within a community. Mumbaza, what suggestions for solutions do we have from the Board?"

"Well, what has been fed upwards from the state representatives is that the low-output and non-active civilians should be given a fair chance to take part in the community, but it won't be within their existing communities. There are discussions about civilian exchanges between communities, but the representatives believe that if it was known to the rest of the community that the new civilians were also low-output or non-active, then it would cause more problems. One other solution came from Thor Hammond of Virgin Red Bull. They have recently reopened the Lunar Project and are able to provide over fifty thousand new jobs. The variety of skills is large enough that they will consider taking on a percentage of low-output or non-active civilians from each state and provide new homes for them on Moon."

"Would Virgin Red Bull take on full responsibility for the move?" asked Emperor Zheng, who was reconstituted as the rightful emperor of China, Taiwan and Japan just before the end of the Great War. One who had never taken to the new non-capitalist arrangements, he was always prudent with considerations of responsibilities.

"Yes, it appears so. They have not enjoyed a good rapport with the people and would like to take this opportunity to be seen contributing to the community. It would also put all their Lunar Crafts into good use."

"I have heard that even though their Lunar Crafts have not been used since the Great War, they have still kept them in good condition," added Prince Mohamed, who was openly known to be good friends with Thor Hammond.

"Yes, that is right, Mohamed. Blue Planet engineers have visited the hangar in Scotland and were very impressed with the efforts they have put in it. The crafts look almost brand new, with all safety checks up to date. They have been using the crafts to bring their construction engineers and equipment onto Moon to re-start the development projects."

"So, they are going ahead with the project regardless of whether they get the civilians?" asked Emperor Zheng again.

"Yes, Zheng. The development project is planned in phases at the moment. If they do not get the civilians, then they will stop at phase five. Otherwise, the full-development goes up to phase twelve, which will take two years to complete."

"And what does Phase twelve cover?" asked Prince Mohamed, warming up to the idea now.

"Fully equipped residences on Near Side for all workers, including all mandatory living facilities; grocery centres, gyms, clinics and so forth. On Far Side, they are planning to create the best holiday resort with all the trimmings. Initial calculations show that applications for a holiday there will be at a minimum of two thousand activity credits." The last statement was greeted by a loud intake of breath from the Royal Committee.

"Start saving credits, people!" King Johannes exclaimed with a whistle.

"Sounds like Virgin Red Bull is aiming high, as always," added Queen Silvia, who started thinking of official reasons for her to test out the Lunar holiday resort in two years.

"If everything is already in place, Mumbaza, has Virgin Red Bull discussed this with the state representatives and has it been filtered down to the civilians in discussions?" asked Queen Catherine, keen to pull the conversation back to the practicalities.

"Actually, yes. There are already many civilians who have volunteered to participate and where the numbers of volunteers are low, the state representatives are sure that they will be able to recruit more."

"In that case, they have my vote," Queen Catherine affirmed, glad that the solution seems to be a good one.

"If we are all happy to proceed with the voting for this point, then let's see some hands for those who are happy for Virgin Red Bull to proceed as discussed."

Unsurprisingly, the decision was unanimous. Royal Committee members were glad for a simple solution that didn't involve a citizens-wide voting, as the arrangements for those are tedious and time consuming. They were also mentally making arrangements to save their activity credits for a Lunar holiday, distracting themselves from the meeting. The murmurs across the room could be heard again.

"Let's try and concentrate, Royals. The next point on the agenda is the tender process for Kagami."

The room went quiet again, with all eyes looking towards Mumbaza.

"Each firm has employed different methods to gain ideas for the tender, some involving the citizens, some are just internal within the firms. At this point, the public competitions are unsurprisingly gaining the most attention. No bad press so far and only excitement and positive reactions."

"Which is the way it should be," King Johannes could not help remarking, gaining an eye roll from Queen Catherine.

"Since things are moving smoothly, Silvia has suggested that her office continue monitoring the situation and will report in monthly," King Mumbaza said, looking at Queen Silvia, who in turn gave the room an assuring nod.

An echo of "agreed" spread in the room as the murmuring began again.

"If there isn't any other business, we'll end today's meeting here. Thanks everyone," King Mumbaza managed to get himself heard as the Royal Committee started dispersing. Prince Mohamed moved to catch Queen Catherine at the door, aware that she had been catching his glances throughout the meeting.

"Cate, would you like some company home?"

"Oh," she remarked. "That's ok. Brend is waiting downstairs." She glanced away, so as not to meet his eye. Their relationship was publicly known after all.

"Of course," he responded with a chuckle. "He wouldn't be a very good boyfriend if he wasn't."

In an even smaller voice she said, "I don't think he sees himself as my boyfriend."

Pretending to ignore the last statement, Prince Mohamed moved the conversation on. "Would you live on Moon, Cate? I don't mean holiday at the resort. I am thinking about staying with the civilians on Near Side to understand how it is to be up there."

"You know, I hadn't considered that, though it would probably be the right thing to do. Having a few of the Royal Committee on Moon might show the civilians going there that it is not, how shall I put it...the dumps."

"The lack of sun during dark periods or the lack of night during bright periods might be uncomfortable at first, but humans adjust easily to new environments. We just have to see about moving your museum over," he ended with a wink.

Smiling now, she said, "Let me think about it, Mohamed. I think it's a good idea, with or without my museum. I'll let you know soon."

He nodded, not taking his eyes off her as she made her way into the elevator, deep in thought.

chapter 4

It was rare to see two Royals out at a public venue, especially for dinner, but Prince Mohamed and Queen Catherine were deep in conversation and seemed unconcerned with the stares from the other dinner patrons. Despite Blue Planet's efforts to remove formalities and protocols from all Royal Committee members, they were still easily recognisable in public and generally revered. Citizens never seemed to be able to uphold their end of the bargain for a more equal standing amongst all. The Royals had already stripped themselves of all traditions and customs, acting purely as representatives or puppets to the people, and still their mere presence commanded attention.

Queen Catherine had decided to move to Moon for a year, to show support for the civilians and to encourage positive thoughts about the comforts of a life there. Prince Mohamed would be heading this mission, as they called it, with Queen Silvia and King Johannes joining the party too. It would be over a year more before they would travel to Moon, but arrangements were already underway.

"Actually, Cate, there is something personal that I would like to ask you please. If that is ok."

"Sure," she responded, glad that the restaurant was dark enough to conceal her emotions.

"I have been meeting up quite frequently with Dr. Coughin as I am intrigued with his work. He spoke about a part of his work that I just wanted to find out if you were aware of...and what you thought."

"What part of his work are you talking about?" Queen Catherine was relieved that the question was about Coughin's work and not her, after all.

"Well, he said that in all his surgeries, he worked with a new anesthesia technique that allows patients to dream a specific moment of their lives. He said that if the moment was a calm and happy one, the recovery was quicker."

Queen Catherine nodded for him to continue.

"Did he use that technique on you? Do you remember how it felt?"

"Yes, and it was very pleasant. I had selected an event from childhood that I'm sure didn't last more than five minutes, but somehow, they managed to stretch it to the entire procedure. It actually made the procedure feel really quick."

"That's great..." Prince Mohamed responded, but he seemed away in his own thoughts.

After a moment of silence, Queen Catherine pressed, "Why did you ask? Is there anything untoward about the procedure?"

"No," he exclaimed, perhaps a little too loudly. "No, no, not at all. It was something else. So, Nemo also told me that the procedures power themselves. What he meant is that the power for the equipment comes from the energy generated by the patients themselves, namely from the emotions they experience."

"Are you sure? That sounds...far-fetched," she was careful not to insult him.

"I doubted it too, but then he showed me the reports, videos and equipment. The thing is, he can't really explain the science behind it, but he has been using that technique for all the procedures, humans and primates, and it works."

"If it works that well, it should be looked at more closely. The possibilities in making use of this are...endless," Queen Catherine whispered the last word as the reality hit her. "Why didn't he tell me about it before or even after the procedure?"

"It seems that there wasn't any additional risk as it was just part of all the equipment and procedure as explained to patients."

"Where did they…no, how did they…actually, where did they collect the energy from the patient?"

"It is through the attachment for the chip. During the procedure, when the patient is having the chip implanted to the nerve, the chip is still connected to the machine that is running the procedure. The impulses that the brain sends through the chip are seen as some sort of electricity to the machines and as soon as that was recognised, Nemo reconfigured the computer to also collect...mine this power. When he first used this on the primates, he tried out different dreams to bring on different emotions. That was when he found that happy emotions make the best recovery, but it seems that anger or stress emotions generate the most energy."

"That is fascinating! We should set Nemo up with a Blue Planet laboratory before anyone else gets hold of this discovery, don't you think?"

"That was my thought exactly. Thanks, Cate. I thought I was being silly about reacting so excitedly about this. I'm glad that you agree."

"Why don't we work this into the plan for the four of us whilst on Moon. If we set Nemo up with a laboratory soon, then we can set-up a routine for daily reports whilst we are on Moon."

"Do you feel that this will somehow come into use very soon in the future? Perhaps to have something to do with Kagami?"

Queen Catherine could just nod. She was always a practical woman, never relying on instincts, but it was her instincts alone that led this now, and she felt out of her depths.

When they presented the case to the rest of the Royal Committee, it was only out of formality that Dr. Coughin was invited to make a full presentation, after which the Royal Committee had no doubt that it was a good decision to have this research within Blue Planet. It was only a couple of days later that Dr. Coughin's laboratory was moved to one of Blue Planet's main research centres, with newer equipment set-up for his arrival. Dr. Dahl, now using her full efforts to support Dr. Coughin's work, remained part of his team in this new arrangement, slowly phasing out her work on migraines. She knew that this would be a better investment for her career.

Chapter 5

As Prince Mohamed travelled through the city, anxious to get an update from Dr. Coughin, he smiled to himself as he thought about his own future, how he would be heading to Moon in about a year's time. *We are travelling from Earth to Moon freely, and yet, I am still chauffeured around in a car, that has four wheels and works on electricity and a little petroleum,* he thought to himself. *Our writers had the imagination for a greater future, but here we are, proving them wrong. At least we are finally going to make use of Moon, and we have surpassed all expectations with the privatisation of Earth with the creation of Blue Planet Inc. For better or worse, we have made the bed that we are sleeping in.*

Prince Mohamed stared contentedly out of his window, letting the meaningless neon lights left from the capitalist days blur his vision, creating streaks of brightness and darkness, patterns of the old ways. They were only maintained now for nostalgia and a sense of aesthetics.

When the peak of the Great War had devastated Earth's population down to just one percent of what it used to be, wiping out whole countries, world leaders came together with a temporary measure to save what was left. This desperate action was so effective that when things had stabilised, citizens pushed for establishing the corporate democratic arrangement to govern all of humanity under the banner of Blue Planet Inc., creating the Royal Committee as its governess. The outcome of that saw the re-proportioning of facilities, trades, careers, work and life, resulting in the cities getting less and less populated whilst communities reinvented themselves. They created a balanced space for the right amount of doctors, nurses, teachers, engineers, farmers, artists, and writers, with Blue Planet acting as central government; purely there to find the right people for any gaps there were within a community.

Arriving at the laboratory, he was surprised to find Queen Catherine already there and in deep conversation with Dr. Coughin and Dr. Dahl. He was quietly pleased to find that Brend was nowhere in sight.

"Good evening, everyone," he greeted the others, trying to hide the excitement and curiosity in his voice.

"Mohamed, it's been a few months," exclaimed Dr. Coughin as he greeted the Prince like an old friend, with an arm around his shoulders.

"Come and join us. We have just been talking about the possibility of Cate bringing her own Coughin machine to Moon."

"It is ready to be used, safely?" blurted Prince Mohamed, unable to contain his emotions anymore.

Smiling, Dr. Dahl responded instead. "Yes. It seems we have passed all the health and safety tests that your Blue Planet regulators have thrown at us. We have even had citizen representatives here to witness a pre-launch presentation and everything seems to be in order."

"It is better than that, Mohamed," Dr. Coughin interjected, beaming. "The citizen representatives have suggested that we roll out personal units that people would be able to use at home, to make and store their own energy. We never thought of that! That is why you always need focus groups!"

"Whoah...can we do that? Cate?" Prince Mohamed looked to Queen Catherine for an explanation, but she just smiled and nodded at him.

"It won't be so soon. We expect the mass production to begin over a year from now, but it means that we have the general approval to make a few customised units now."

"And Mohamed," added Queen Catherine, "this here was the unit that Nemo used during my surgery. He says that since it was only used by me—it seems he has a few other units that he uses for others—he has pimped it up for me." She couldn't help whispering the last sentence with a little giggle. Such a crude and old phrase, but yet appropriate, she had thought.

She had not known but Prince Mohamed was a little jealous, feeling left out from it all. He fought the urge to throw a tantrum, to ask Nemo for a chip implant. The actions of a Royal will take time to wear out.

"There is still the small issue of the attachment, Mohamed," Queen Catherine pulled his thoughts back to the room.

"Yes, we have scheduled Cate in for the minor surgery to attach what I call the adapter, which will then connect easily to her sleeping machine here."

"Oh, another surgery for Cate?" Prince Mohamed asked as he started to feel embarrassed inwardly for his selfish thoughts earlier.

"Don't worry, Mohamed. It is all very straightforward and it'll be done before you both leave for Moon. Actually, we need to ask you an important question."

"Sure, what is it?" he looked around and paused at Queen Catherine's gentle smile. Her eyes twinkled with the suggestion of further news to share.

"We would like to give you some basic medical and technical training, so that you may be Cate's supervisor, managing her well-being when she uses the machine."

"Me? Really?" he asked, feeling unsure about the responsibility. Ever since Blue Planet Inc. was formed, the Royals never really had the chance to assert any power or be responsible for anything. All decisions were publicly discussed and agreed upon before the Royal Committee took action on them or delegated the work to the Board of Directors.

"Yes, Mohamed, I would be comforted to know that you are the one supervising me when I'm using the machine," added Queen Catherine.

"With your background in science and your past medical training, even though you did not practice after you joined the Royal Committee, we are all confident with your skills and knowledge," Dr. Coughin tried to assure Prince Mohamed further.

"Ok. I'm…I'm honoured," he finally managed to reply after a moment's pause. "I would have one requirement, though."

"What is that?" asked Queen Catherine and Dr. Coughin simultaneously.

"If at any point I feel that we should not be using the machine, my decision must be respected. As long as it is only Cate and me, then my decision on the usage is final."

Dr. Coughin looked towards Queen Catherine, silently asking for her opinion as she turned to Prince Mohamed and nodded.

"I agree. If you have to be responsible for my well-being, then I think that is a fair request."

"Great, that's all settled then." Freya stepped in to take over on the logistical arrangements with Cate as Nemo started scheduling training sessions for Mohamed.

Life on Moon won't be boring after all, thought Prince Mohamed as they worked through the night.

The next year flew by as arrangements were finalised for the mass migration of tens of thousands of people to Moon. Queen Catherine spent many quiet nights with Brend, assuring him that she will keep well, making plans for Brend's first trip over to make their first holiday to Far Side. She was quietly uncertain whether being that close to Prince Mohamed was going to affect her relationship with Brend, but she weighed the decision and thought that it was probably worth it, whatever happens. Living on Moon was a great opportunity for her to prove her importance within the Royal Committee. She was also in a unique position with her chip implant, a position that gave her the upper hand in any situations that might crop up with the Coughin machines. She knew that she needed Prince Mohamed's scientific knowledge on her side and she was more than glad that he proved himself to be a more formidable business partner than she had imagined.

She felt that there was quite a strong sexual tension between them, but was both disappointed and glad that he had not acted on it, knowing that she would not have been able to resist. She considered that she might not be his type, but failed to recall him with any women. Even Qamari, his PA, who could have any man or woman on the Royal Committee and Board of Directors, managed a tender but seemingly platonic relationship with Prince Mohamed.

chapter 6

Moon, the new frontier *for mankind*, thought Queen Catherine to herself as she made her way out of the space shuttle with Sarah, her PA, in tow. Her first reactions were that it had felt no different than a very long flight on Earth. There was perhaps a bit more apprehension from all passengers at take-off and at leaving the atmosphere. In reality, if the flight captain had not told them of each transition point, they would probably not have realised it anyway. In truth, Moon is not a new frontier for mankind. Before the Great War, when capitalism had flourished and the worth of humanity was based purely on money—paper notes printed that differed from country to country—many had come to Moon in an attempt to make more money, to break the market with something new.

Red Bull were the market leaders then, as the economy gurus had called them. That was before they were asked to justify their worth as a corporation to communities and citizens, before the public had realised that they were exploiting people's curiosity like many other corporations. They all claimed to be inspirational and knowledge driven, when what they were actually doing was distracting people from the bigger issues on Earth. That was when they called in the help of Virgin to create a partnership that would help them earn back the trust of citizens. It helped, but they were still pressured by the people more than the other corporations.

Blue Planet had been established to stop the capitalist nonsense that had provoked the Great War and the many wars before then. Neither did it advocate for the historical concept of communism. With Blue Planet, the people believed that they had found a strong balance, bringing in the ability that corporations have to react and change quickly with the just organisation of a democracy.

The concentrated efforts from one office, the Blue Planet office, did indeed help disperse the ailments of humanity, like poverty, starvation, and most importantly, war. Greed, though it could never be completely abolished, had been reduced to being a petty notion. Output credit was changed to suit the level of impact a job had on its community based on how much effort and time it took. This change promoted a transparency in work and benefits that had never been possible before. Blue Planet was then able to concentrate its efforts to relocate and assist communities that had previously suffered from environmental difficulties or a bad economical state, slowly reducing the rich-poor divide by ultimately removing the source of the problem, the capitalist economy. Realising that there could never be a perfect system, citizens were still able to appreciate all the positive changes that Blue Planet had brought, which now brought them back to Moon again.

Queen Catherine and Sarah were to meet the other Royal Committee members at the Blue Planet Arrival Hall and were led through a glass corridor. Looking out into the main arrival hall, they were both shocked to see the number of people being organised into groups. The main arrival hall was full, with a sea of bobbing heads and shoulder sacks. Queen Catherine realised with amazement that most people had not experienced such over-crowdedness since the Great War. Twenty-four years was a long time and those who were around for the Great War would have forgotten what it was like. Most people who were under thirty would have only seen it in pictures, on the history channel.

They stared just long enough to realise that there was an order to the chaos below with Virgin Red Bull staff and Blue Planet officers dotted around the building, ushering people into various exits. Queen Catherine and Sarah continued to walk, both glad that they were travelling on Blue Planet terms.

I met your mother in the main arrival hall on Moon, where we had all arrived from a tireless journey, excited for a change in our lives. I had stared across the room at a young lady with bright red hair. I heard the people around her call her Magdalena and I made a mental note of it. I was very shy and I felt slightly embarrassed, as I loved how traditional her name was.

I moved through the crowd to try and get to her side surreptitiously, drawn like a moth to a light. The arrival hall was full of immigrants like us, who were tired from the long journey and were clutching all their worldly belonging close to their bodies. I did not care for mine.

We were all scared. Scared that people would nick our things, scared that we would find Moon uninhabitable, scared that it was all a massive scam by Blue Planet. But for a moment, I had no care in the world as I was distracted by this red-haired girl.

As I got closer to her, I could smell her shampoo. She kept her hair long, like a badge of traditionality. Bright red hair that stood out in the crowd like fire. She smelt of hibiscus. I remember very clearly that when I closed my eyes, I could see and smell her hair, the strands blending into petals, soft and graceful.

"Please," I heard her say, which snapped me out of my reverie. Her voice was like an angel's.

I had not realised that I had gotten so close that I was right next to her and all I could manage was a, "Huh?" Clearly my verbal skills were not as eloquent as my writing.

"Can you help me, please?" she asked and I said ok. At that

moment, I remembered all the things that my parents warned me of. Single girls will try and trick you into marriage so that they won't be kicked out of the community or forced into hard labour. There's no such thing as love at first sight and you shouldn't trust anyone, especially single girls who were alone.

"I'm sorry, I am intruding and you don't even know me," she said to me as I considered all the past advice my parents had given me.

"It's ok," I said. "My name is Horace. Now that you know my name, you know me." I realised that I was smiling like a freak and I was surprised that she was still standing there talking to me.

She smiled back at me and made my heart melt.

"All families please remain together. Singles will be selected first for work allocations." *The speakers in the arrival hall blasted that message every five minutes and at that moment, it served as a warning for me to get back to my parents, but I knew that I couldn't leave her.*

"My name is Magdalena. Nice to meet you," she said with a shy smile and a slight curtsy. Curtsy! What a traditionalist! I knew then that my mother would love her.

"What help do you need, Magdalena?" I asked, knowing the answer and secretly hoping that I was right.

"I am single," she told me, swallowing the last word as if it was a sin.

We didn't speak after that as I took her bag from her and led her back to where my parents were waiting. They knew when they saw her that we had decided to be together, to be a family and they never stopped us. I guess they had fallen in love with her too.

That was how I met your mother—it was love at first sight.

"Cate, over here," Queen Silvia called out from the bar where King Johannes and Prince Mohamed were already with beverages in hand.

"Did you all see the chaos downstairs?"

They all nodded as they sipped their drinks, standing in a simple lounge created with simple lines of concrete and glass. Though the furniture was obviously of good quality and design, the simplicity of the room made it look like an old army bunker with only the necessities. Even the servers were dressed in drab grey uniforms.

"What would you like, Cate, and you, Sarah?" asked Prince Mohamed. Having given their orders to the bar staff, Prince Mohamed assured Queen Catherine that the organisation for the relocation of the people on Moon is good.

"We are just not used to seeing so many people altogether anymore," he said.

"Now, who's excited about seeing our new palaces?" King Johannes exclaimed dramatically as the others cringed at his lack of tact.

"What? Come on, don't be spoilsports. Let's enjoy this long business trip of ours. I hope they managed to install the Jacuzzi I asked for," he added with a wink. Only his PA, Thomas, giggled, gaining a direct wink from King Johannes as if they were sharing an inside joke.

Ronaldo, Queen Silvia's PA, stepped in and saved the moment as he announced that their transportation was ready and that he knew the way, if they would follow him.

Grateful and keen to get to their new homes, they downed their drinks and moved, unaware of the small entourage behind them who were managing their carry-on baggage. The rest of their things had already been brought over and installed a few days earlier, under strict instructions by their PAs.

Chapter 7

THE CITIZENS' EXPERIENCE IN settling into their new lives on Moon could not have been more different from the Royal Committee members'. Despite the determination from citizens and Royal Committee alike to banish any sort of class separations between individuals, the Royals nevertheless still enjoyed a certain level of additional courtesy from organisations run by the Board of Directors wherever they went. Constitution or not, it was not possible for citizens to monitor personal perks that were extended to the Royal Committee members, when selected citizens enjoyed the same occasionally.

All the buildings on Moon were linked up together, creating a large complex, like a city shielded in glass. A manageable temperature of just over freezing was maintained in the "outdoors" whilst "indoors" temperatures were kept at twenty-three degrees centigrade. To help with the dark and bright periods and to maintain some uniformity with Earth living, every room was installed with basic lights that mimic natural light and blackout blinds. All communal areas and streets and "outdoors" had automated lights, coming on for twelve hours of the day, from 07:00 to 19:00 to mimic daytime during dark periods. During bright periods, Moon citizens were advised to remain indoors when possible.

Although this initially seemed to be a weird experience, most people adapted to the environment easily, glad that they had maintained Earth's twenty-four hour system. On days when the satellite was clearly visible from Earth, the artificial lights from Moon painted a low ebb of illuminations, like dying glow-worms on a stone. It was a constant reminder to those on Earth, of the progress on Moon and of those who had relocated there.

The most remarkable piece of engineering on Moon, though, were the gravity plates. Known officially as Tabulae Galileo-Newton, they were invented by Virgin Red Bull scientists before the Great War. They were what prompted Blue Planet to agree to development plans on Moon for the first human settlers. Scientists had for the longest time considered making Moon habitable for humans, but the issue of gravity seemed to consistently be a problem. Physiologically, it was impossible for human bodies to be able to cope living with a different level of gravity for long periods of time. It was predicted that it would initially cause physical ailments and then, through generations, mutations would appear to adapt to the environment. Such mutations would make it unadvisable to return to Earth's gravity. Another problem was presented by the mascons on Moon, pockets of uneven gravity throughout the satellite. That was until the Tabula Galileo-Newton was invented.

After the Great War, scientists managed to improve the engineering of the gravity plates to the point where they are able to manipulate the level of gravity in an area of up to the size of a football pitch with just four strategically placed plates, whilst still keeping the gravity even.

The Royal Committee members settled comfortably into a large bungalow built at the edge of the shielded compound for them. The bungalow had four large bedrooms, four large study rooms, and communal rooms for their leisure, living area, kitchen, and dining. Their PAs were put up in bunker style accommodations, which were the same as other citizens on moon, but in a building just a few steps away from the bungalow. Although their rooms were the same as the other citizens' on Moon, they each had a comfortably sized study in addition to the communal kitchen and living rooms.

Queen Catherine and Prince Mohamed's study rooms were allocated next to each other as Queen Catherine's Coughin machine was set up in her study, a room decorated very similarly to her office on Earth. All her museum relics, as they were nicknamed, were transported over with care and used to redecorate her new study and home for at least the next year, if not two. On entering her new study for the first time, she smiled at the great job that Sarah had done in decorating and thought of how intimately Sarah actually knew her.

She paced around her study, taking in the new environment, slowly realising that the slight feeling of unease she was having was due to what she had initially thought was a large window. Staring closely, it was actually a large monitor that displayed the view of a tree, grass, birds chirping, but most importantly the bright daylight. That screen seemed to juxtapose the artificial lighting in the room. Sarah, who had just walked in at that moment, sensed the discomfort in Queen Catherine.

"Is it the screen, Cate?"

Catherine nodded, still staring in disbelief.

Smiling, Sarah said, "It actually looked weird even from the photographs that I was sent from the designers. They realised that not everyone likes it, so they built in a second option with it."

Sarah walked towards the left of the screen where there was a wall control panel, taking her time to work out the new controls.

"Oh by the way, you can upload any video images to the screen and there are quite a few presets too. But…" she paused just as she clicked a switch that started the mechanics of the screen to whirr and slowly flipping it up, storing it away to present an actual window.

"Ta dah!" she said with a smile.

It was a real window, looking out onto the side of the bungalow, facing a small road and the PAs' bunkers. There were beautiful potted trees laid to enhance the rocky surface of Moon, and with the lighting from the outside, it felt a little more natural.

"That's much better," whispered Queen Catherine.

Sarah smiled, glad that she had predicted Queen Catherine's response well.

"Cate, here is our communications device, which is my favourite part of being on Moon," she said as she handed over what looked like a beautiful necklace with a small spiral locket that was completely made out of carbon fibre in black chrome.

"If you don't like the colour, I can get you another one in gold or platinum."

"No, this is beautiful. How does it work?"

"Great." Sarah moved to help Queen Catherine put it on, and then she showed her the button at the base of the spiral design.

"If you touch it once, you'll feel a light buzz," she motioned for Queen Catherine to try.

At that moment, Sarah held out her wrist, showing Queen Catherine an identical locket hanging off her bracelet for the first time. It vibrated quietly.

"This works anywhere on Moon as long as we are both within the shielded area of the artificial atmosphere. If I feel the buzz, I will just come to you as soon as I can."

Queen Catherine nodded in acknowledgement.

"If you want to speak with me, you just need to hold down

the button a little longer, until the vibrations stop. There is a built in speaker, so you can just speak normally."

Again, Queen Catherine tried it, but she was surprised when she couldn't hear anything from Sarah's locket.

"I have a semi-permanent earpiece fitted in my right ear, so I hear your messages without additional efforts and with full privacy."

"That is genius. Whose design is this?" asked Queen Catherine, though from her blushing, Sarah realised that she knew the answer already. "Brend?" asked Queen Catherine more quietly now, and Sarah nodded in acknowledgement.

"I have an earpiece for you too, if you would like to have a two-way conversation."

Sarah approached Queen Catherine's necklace again and showed her how to detach a small clear earpiece from the top of the spiral locket. Queen Catherine placed it on her finger, admiring the sleekness of the design before placing it in her ear. The earpiece moulded with the inner ear perfectly and as Queen Catherine went to look at a mirror, she was pleased to find that it was not visible at all. Like contact lenses, you would need to stare very hard to see it.

"Do I press it again to stop?"

"Yes."

Queen Catherine spent another few minutes replacing the earpiece a few times before she walked to the end of the room and motioned for Sarah to remain where she was. Placing the earpiece in, she buzzed Sarah and asked in a whisper, "Who else has this?"

"No one, Cate. Brend told me that this was his special present for us for Moon."

"Who else knows about this?"

"No one," Sarah replied, as she started to sense the importance of this object. She had initially thought that it was just another gadget that would allow them to work more efficiently, but this could be useful in many situations. "Ah, you reminded me of another of its function," Sarah added.

"Tell me," Queen Catherine replied, still using the intercom surreptitiously. To anyone looking, she would appear to be standing by her window, taking in the new view she had.

Sarah, now moving to tidy up one of Queen Catherine's bookshelves, explained that all their communications were automatically recorded and the archive storage is up to a year. If they required it, the recordings can easily be downloaded for reviewing. It was all secure and protected, with only Sarah and Queen Catherine having any access. Even though Brend had set it up in the first place, Sarah had reset all the passwords to protect it for just the two of them.

"Thanks Sarah, you've been amazing in our move. I think you deserve a break. I'm going to rest and probably not do much for a day or two. I'll buzz you when I'm up and about."

Queen Catherine turned to smile at Sarah as she gave her a cheeky wink before Sarah left the bungalow. Cate was glad to have some time to herself to settle into her new environment.

Not surprisingly, Queen Catherine, Prince Mohamed, Queen Silvia and King Johannes stayed in their bungalow for the next few days, just taking in their new home whilst getting to know each other better as housemates. No work was done and they took turns cooking, telling stories and using every new piece of equipment that had been installed in the bungalow, enjoying their time exploring. They left their PAs to their own time and had only the cleaning staff in the bungalow helping them with basic household chores. It seemed like they were on a holiday together, rather than on work relocation.

Our bunkers on Moon were lovely. Many complained that they were smaller than what they were used to on Earth, but your mother and I loved it. With your grandparents, the four of us were allocated a bunker with two simple bedrooms sharing a living and cooking area. Your grandmother was even given a sewing machine so that she could work in the bunker, allowing her to look after your grandfather and work flexibly. She was sewing top quality bathrobes for the resort on Far Side. The furnishings in the bunkers were all standard issue stuff as they would call it. It just meant that they were all the same across Near Side.

As an engineer, I was very happy as I was allocated the job of maintaining the Lunar trucks. They ran by solar power and, when not in use, were parked in the bright period sectors for charging. I had my own garage of tools and I had twenty trucks under my care. The garage was situated not far from our bunkers and I used to just walk to it, taking about fifteen minutes each way.

Your mother worked at the grocery distribution centre, where all sorts of produce were distributed to all citizens on Moon. We were rationed, like on Earth, so there was never a shortage of food for everyone. The only thing we didn't have on Moon was restaurants. There were two canteens on Near Side and we were all allowed to eat there twice a month, but most people just saved the visits for special occasions, like birthdays and anniversaries. Actually, the groceries were better quality on Moon than Earth. In fact, I think we were eating better on Moon than we ever did on Earth.

Anyway, the grocery centre job was the first job your mother had ever done in her life, and I remember her first day, as she was so nervous. You would have been proud of her too, had you been there. Everyone at the grocery centre loved her and loved having her around. She always knew how to make a room light up, even though she is as shy as a dormouse. Have you learnt that saying yet? Do you know what a dormouse is? Oh, have you read Alice in Wonderland? Oh, I always have so many questions for you, but I know that you won't get these letters until you have left the facilities on Kagami. By then, maybe we won't be around anymore, or maybe you won't want to know about us. At least they've always been upfront about that, telling us that this arrangement avoids distractions and any emotional setbacks, though I cannot see how it would.

Well, let's get back to our time on Moon. Although we lived like a married couple, your mother and I were still virgins in that first year. I'm imagining that you are squirming as you read this and complaining, "Dad, shut up, you're embarrassing me." Oh, how beautiful you are in your photographs, Sun. I can only dream of spending time together as a family, just the three of us, but I hope that you will always know and remember how much we love you.

We were just happy to be a family, finally, living on Near Side. Your grandfather was looked after well by your grandmother and us, and we were not under any stress about under-performing or having concerned community members breathing down our necks. For most of that first year on Moon, we spent time as a normal family, enjoying work and life.

chapter 8

"HEY MUMBAZA, IF YOU keep insisting on showing us the beautiful view from Blue Planet headquarters, you know we won't be listening to a word that anyone says, right?" King Johannes piped up as the Royal Committee settled down for their first meeting together after the four relocated to Moon. It had been just over four months now and the sight of sunshine and blue skies from the video feed was proving to be distracting for all of them on Moon. The rest were just glad that King Johannes had voiced it for them.

"Sorry," apologised King Mumbaza as he moved the camera to face a duller part of the room. "Can everyone move around so our colleagues on Moon may see all of us?" he added, ushering the rest of the Royal Committee into an impromptu seating arrangement.

"Thanks, Mumbaza," Queen Silvia acknowledged, happy to take control of the communications from Moon. As everyone settled, she continued, "We have been here four months now and we are happy to report that it has been a really smooth transition for us and that we are fully settled in now. The citizens have been organised very well by Virgin Red Bull and we would like to pass on a word of congratulations to Thor Hammond and his teams for putting all this into action. It has been amazing."

King Mumbaza nodded and as he looked around the room he said, "We are glad to hear that Silvia and we have noted to commend Thor Hammond and his teams appropriately. Do you have anything else to add to your report?"

"Yes. We have found our work as Royal Committee on Moon to be most fulfilling so far. We have been fortunate in this situation to have direct contact with most citizens. Though still in the initial stages, the four of us have decided to take turns to visit various work areas and bunkers, to gain the trust of citizens here. When interviewed, citizens were frank and direct in their approach with us, which we all feel is very different from the reception we get on Earth. Most citizens here are grateful for the second chance in being a part of a community, and their main fear before arriving on Moon was mostly a fear of surviving. Four months in for most, this fear has subsided to nearly nothing and the new communities are flourishing with many new marriages and reports of our first pregnancies," Queen Silvia ended with a nod.

Applause broke out from the Earth delegates as the Moon delegates sat smiling, proud of their achievements. Queen Silvia, Prince Mohamed, and Queen Catherine had all made at least one visit each to the citizens' bunkers and work areas, but King Johannes was still just enjoying his relocation as a holiday. The three knew that making this announcement at the committee would change things for Johannes as he would have to be seen to be pulling his weight. It wouldn't be long before he would make his first visit.

"Thank you, Silvia. It is great work that you are all doing there. Keep it up and maybe you'll be able to help us develop stronger ties with citizens on Earth, too. Silvia, and if you and Ronaldo could work on the press releases for Earth on what you've found so far, that would be great. Thank you."

"Ok. Next item on the list is the Coughin machines. Cate, Mohamed, I have a report from Dr. Coughin that he thinks that enough time has passed for Cate to have settled physically to the new environment and that you may start using the machine there when you are comfortable."

King Mumbaza paused to give Queen Catherine and Prince Mohamed a chance to absorb the information. Both turned to look at each other and then turned to face the camera with a glisten of excitement in their eyes. "Thank you, Mumbaza. We will report back as soon as we have made our first attempt. I am sure that Mohamed will keep an open relay with Dr. Coughin during the first attempt, so you will receive a report from Dr. Coughin as well."

Prince Mohamed nodded in agreement.

"Thank you. Also, Nemo informed us that he now has a team of twenty citizens using the Coughin machines as their primary outputs. These twenty volunteers will remain as the initial test subjects for the next three months, after which, we will regroup to consider widening the usage to centres around Earth. Cate, your own usage and report on it will affect this decision heavily as well as help generate positive messages for it."

"Of course, Mumbaza. We will be thorough with our report."

"Finally, Silvia, if you would like to take the last point, we will have an update on the progress of the tender process for Kagami."

"Thanks, Mumbaza," Queen Silvia said as she tapped on her tablet, bringing up the information she needed for the report.

"Well, let's start with those who are using public input first. Surprisingly, only five organisations have done so and only one is in the form of a competition. Not surprisingly, that is Virgin Red Bull, and the incentive is that the winner and his/her family get to live on Far Side for a year if the tender gets selected." Queen Silvia had to stop for a break here whilst the room applauded at that last statement. "There are obviously justifications that Virgin Red Bull will have to make if their tender application gets selected, but they have already discussed this with our legal team and have found that it won't be difficult to get permission for this, as the winner would have ultimately contributed so much to his or her community to justify such a high credit expenditure. In theory, if the tender goes to a single person's idea, that person should really be off the hook for any further contributions to the community for the rest of his or her life. Any questions so far?"

"We've all seen the campaigns and have heard about the high interest from citizens, but do you have any reports on how it is actually faring, especially in comparison to the other four public campaigns?" Queen Sia asked. No doubt the rest of the Royal Committee were thinking about her close relationship with Thor Hammond. Unlike Prince Mohamed's friendship with Thor, Queen Sia's wasn't just a platonic one.

"I was just getting to that, Sia," Queen Silvia couldn't hide the note of impatience in her voice. "The other four public campaigns provide no incentives to participants. The only provisions are the resources of the organisation—full access to all the technology, manpower, research materials, anything really that the participants might want to make use of from the organisation. These resources are currently publicly available insofar as that one would have to apply to the organisation for access, stating the reason for access and how it might benefit the community. These applications have been primarily handled by the organisations themselves, but randomly regulated by Blue Planet to ensure as high a level of fairness as possible. However, for the tender applications, all one has to do is to submit a vague idea that links to the resources of the organisation and they will be given access based on the relevance."

"I would assume then that this would prove popular amongst post-graduate researchers," suggested Queen Sia.

"Yes, that is right, Sia. The four organisations have been managing a low-level of communications for their campaigns, which is why we haven't seen or heard much, and most of the interests they have received are from universities or post-graduate students directly. However, they have since requested that Blue Planet handle the communications, making it a fairer system for all four. Basically, they would like us to announce that these four organisations are recruiting for tender ideas and to help citizens consider, we will have links to the various resources that citizens will be given access to."

"Sorry Silvia, but can you tell us what the four organisations are? I really have not seen any communications from their campaigns so far," King Johannes prodded from Moon, smirking because Queen Silvia had told him off just before the meeting about not participating enough in citizens' affairs.

"Of course, Johannes."

Those in the makeshift boardroom on Moon couldn't help giggling whilst Queen Silvia proceeded with her report with a straight face, but her hands were gesturing rudely at King Johannes, just out of view of the video.

"They are Cyberity, EcoBio, Walkabout, and Cambridge. The communications for this will go public tomorrow, so you can all follow and look through the resources for each there."

Queen Silvia went on to speak about the other organisations that were working internally to come up with tender ideas. Most were still at the brainstorming phase, trying to shortlist a few key ideas to work with. Many of the themes were similar too, involving exploring and populating Kagami. Even with centuries of imagination on what humanity would do if a new habitable planet were found, in reality, not many people dared to think of it in realistic terms.

After the meeting closed, those on Moon continued sitting around in their living area, taking in what was discussed.

Queen Silvia and Queen Catherine had inadvertently started organising their next citizen visits, when King Johannes took the hint.

"Alright, I will come with you on your next visit."

"Really?" asked Catherine, not even trying to hide her surprise.

"Yes, and it's only to shut all of you up. I signed up for a holiday, not for more work than on Earth." Though Johannes tried to maintain a certain level of aloofness, his curiosity piqued him and the others could see that he was slowly coming around to the idea of understanding the Moon communities better.

"That's great, Johannes. Whatever your reason for doing it, I'm just glad you're doing it," said Mohamed with a wink to the two women. All three were quietly bemused that their campaign had worked.

Chapter 9

Queen Catherine and Prince Mohamed were working in her study, setting up the Coughin machine for their first attempt on their own. Dr. Coughin was on standby on the communicator, having scheduled in light research work so that he would be made available to help them at a moment's notice.

"How do you think Johannes will react on his first field-trip?" Cate asked, making conversation whilst they were setting up.

"You know, I have a feeling that it will change him."

"What? You think he's going to suddenly grow a heart?" she laughed, glad to be distracted from what they were going to do.

"You never know," suggested Mohamed more seriously. "Johannes has never experienced hardship or mingled with citizens in all his life. The only reason he still holds his role in our Committee is purely because he's good at being in the shadows, not bringing any attention to himself."

"I never thought of it that way, you know." After a brief pause, Queen Catherine added, "You're right, I've never seen Johannes do anything that brings attention to himself publicly. He always keeps his snotty remarks to within our group."

Nodding, Prince Mohamed added with a slight grin, "He might regret his decision to come to Moon. He probably thought that he could just kick back and relax for a year or two. I doubt he ever thought that anyone would be interested in the on-goings on Moon when everything here is controlled by Virgin Red Bull."

Laughing now, Cate said, "If we can get a year's work out of him, it'll be worth it."

The laughter slowly subsided as the tension in the room grew. In the centre of the Queen's study sat the Coughin machine, quiet and daunting. Though beautifully designed with mouldable glass and titanium, it still could not help giving out a sinister feel, like Snow White's glass casket. Both Sarah and Qamari were asked to stay in their own quarters for the night, as Mohamed felt that he would rather be in control without disruption, but both PAs were also asked to be on standby.

"How do you feel, Cate?"

"Oh, I feel great, actually. The last time I was sleeping in the machine, I had the best rest ever, so I am looking forward to it in some ways." She tried to convince herself to remain calm as much as she was trying to convince Mohamed of her confidence in the machine.

"That's great. I guess I am more nervous than you are."

"I think that's understandable, as you are working the machine. Don't worry, I am sure that you are more than capable and I trust you completely," Cate smiled reassuringly at Mohamed as they continued to work.

Queen Catherine, dressed in a body suit that showed off every curve on her body, stepped into the Coughin machine, which looked like a glass bed. The machine was moulded to her body so that she may lie comfortably, fully supported at every part. The mould was made of a jelly-like material that was dense and strong enough to support the body weight but yet springy enough to be comfortable, allowing for slight physical changes. Once she was fully settled, Prince Mohamed made sure that the adaptor at the base of her skull was attached to the receiver on the Coughin machine.

"Comfortable?" he asked.

"Very, actually. You should get one of these beds. They're amazing," she smiled.

"Ok. Now, I would like you to pick a happy moment in your life that you would like to remember whilst you're sleeping."

"Any moment?"

"Yes, any moment. As long as you can recall some part of it, we can work with it."

"Hmmm…ok. Do I have to tell you?"

"Erm…yes. Sorry. Is it a naughty memory?" he asked, blushing for her.

"No, no, no…don't be silly. It's a childhood memory of mine."

"Oh, ok. If you tell me the general happenings of this memory, I can include some key words that the machine will trigger as impulses periodically, so that your thoughts don't stray. It means that you get to experience this happy moment for the entire time you're asleep. This is the new feature that Nemo had upgraded on your machine. The standard machines currently only trigger a release of endorphins. "

"Ok. When I was about five, I think, this was before the Great War, my parents brought me to India for an official state visit. My great-grandmother was still in power, but she had started to delegate visits to other members of our family as she was getting older. My parents decided to make it a long visit. We lived in a remote area in India, with the most beautiful beaches. Anyway, the memory is from that period as I spent most of that month in love with Booboo, my elephant."

"Booboo?"

"Hey, I was five and they allowed me to name him! Anyway, Booboo was a Gaja—that was what they called elephants in that part of India—and he and I spent the most memorable month together."

"That must have been amazing, Cate. I didn't realise that you have actually spent so much time with nature before."

"Yes, I am one of the lucky few who had the chance before the Great War destroyed most of Mother Earth's creations. Of course, things are different now."

"Well, this is your lucky day, lady!" Prince Mohamed put on a show voice to lift the mood. "I am going to send you on a trip back to memory lane, so you may enjoy a night with Booboo!"

They both smiled, calmer and excited now about this first attempt. Prince Mohamed completed the preparations by typing in key words like elephant, India, Booboo and Gaja, which would all be triggered whilst Queen Catherine was asleep. It was amazing how few triggers a mind needs to reimagine an experience.

"Ok, Cate. I'll begin the process now."

"Thanks, Mohamed."

"No problem. I'll be right here with you until I wake you up in three hours' time, as we agreed."

"Perfect. See you later and good night."

He typed in a series of commands to start the process, sending Queen Catherine to sleep. As the machine picked up her life signs, noting that she was moving into sleep, the jelly-like compound started growing, covering more of her body, until she was completely enclosed within it, leaving only her face exposed. The jelly acted to control the temperature of the body whilst providing comfort against bedsores and the risk of deep vein thrombosis. Once the jelly covered the body fully, Mohamed could choose to cover the machine and stand it up, or have the jelly trigger muscle movements in her body for longer sessions, so that the muscles do not get too lax.

A few minutes in, the machine beeped a message, notifying him that Queen Catherine was ready to enter the rapid eye movement (REM) stage, triggering dreaming. Dr. Coughin had managed to develop a method that allowed the user to go directly into REM, surpassing the other stages, saving time.

As Prince Mohamed kept a close eye on the readings provided by the machine of Queen Catherine's life signs, he saw that the first dream triggers were made and that her brainwaves reflected that she was indeed in a happy dream. He then checked the impulse output and was immediately excited to find that she was indeed creating power and that the machine was mining the power as it should.

He took that moment to message Dr. Coughin to inform him that everything was ok and that the machine was running smoothly. The reply was nonchalant, reflecting the confidence that Nemo had with the operation and with Mohamed's abilities.

Going back to the power readings, Prince Mohamed made a mental calculation and realised that the amount of power they would produce in the three hours, will be more than enough to power the bungalow for a whole day. It was incredible to think that sleeping produced that much energy.

Checking himself, as he realised that he must continue to be vigilant, Prince Mohamed kept a close eye on all the readings coming from the machine for the next three hours, until the soft beeping from the control unit told him that the three hours was up. Carefully following his notes all the way, Prince Mohamed took Queen Catherine out of sleep, step-by-step as he had practiced many times with Dr. Coughin. When the machine completely stopped the connection with Queen Catherine's chip, it started to reduce the jelly, whilst allowing the change in temperature to rouse her naturally.

It took another few minutes before Catherine came to completely, but she opened her eyes and smiled directly at Mohamed after a large yawn.

"Unplug me please," she said as she realised that he was still in a bit of a shock, realising that their first attempt had been a complete success.

"Yes, of course." He snapped straight into action, being as gentle as possible.

"How did it go?" she asked, slowly stepping out of the machine.

"Like a dream. It was amazing, Cate. You'll probably find the data boring, but the amount of power you generated in the three hours, it is astounding."

"How astounding?"

"We have enough power in here," he said, caressing the machine like a lover, "to power this bungalow fully for a day. All from three hours of sleep from you."

"Hey, it's not just me. It's you too, and Booboo! Booboo helped a lot," she said, smiling widely now.

"Yes, how were your dreams?"

"Actually, it felt like I only dreamt for a few minutes. The dream was perfect. Booboo was as cheeky as I remembered him to be and the sand and the sea…all so vivid."

"That's amazing," said Prince Mohamed, as he got lost in his own thoughts.

"Mohamed, shouldn't we let Nemo know that we're done here?"

"Huh, what…yes! Definitely," Prince Mohamed hurriedly reached for the computer, realising that he was still somewhat lost in the moment.

Dr. Coughin, happy to hear from them, suggested that they both go and have a good meal and rest. He asked them not to discuss the procedure just yet as the immediacy might cloud their thoughts, but that they should get together the next day, discuss the process and write a report to be published.

As it sounded like good advice, both Prince Mohamed and Queen Catherine tidied up the study and went to get some hot food, after which they bid each other good night and slept soundly, tired from the excitement. Queen Catherine had sent a brief message to Sarah before leaving her study to let her know that everything went well and that she will debrief her in the morning. Comforted that Sarah was on standby as well, Queen Catherine counted her blessings and thought of all those around her whom she trusted.

chapter 10

The success of Queen Catherine's first attempt in the Coughin machine helped Dr. Coughin and the Blue Planet scientists gain further confidence from citizens, especially since the news had spread so quickly on Moon. The report was distributed only three days after the attempt and it was received with much celebration.

Dr. Coughin had already been publishing reports from the usage of the machines with the twenty volunteer test subjects, but somehow it took the involvement of a Royal Committee member to gain the kind of public drive the project had needed.

Encouraged, Blue Planet took this news as a chance to gain further feedback from another citizens focus group, which led to the push for Coughin Centres to be developed and for the manufacturing of personal machines to go forward as well.

Queen Catherine and Prince Mohamed developed a weekly routine using the Coughin machine, slowly increasing the usage time until it became a full seven-hour session. To ensure minimal disruption to their schedules, they held the sessions at night, allowing Cate to sleep in the machine as she would normally. Prince Mohamed also shared the sessions with Sarah and Qamari, so that he could oversee the beginning and end of the sessions while the PAs took three hour shifts each in between to allow him time to sleep.

The organisation of each session was so effective that they were able to increase the frequency of the sessions from once a week to twice a week, before finally settling on a session every other day.

In the few months that followed, Queen Catherine and Prince Mohamed were able to speak about the Coughin machine at their citizen's visits. King Johannes had started participating as promised, and the campaign turned out to be a very successful one for everyone.

Queen Silvia had organised for the four Royals to spend a week at a grocery distribution centre, setting up a small area where they would meet and chat with anyone who had any questions about what they were doing on Moon, or what Blue Planet's current projects were. Since the grocery centre was always open to allow for anyone doing any job on Moon to be able to collect their grocery rations at any time, the Royals took turns so that at least one of them was present all the time as well. King Johannes, being the night owl of the group and always preferring the hours of darkness on Earth, kept the same routine on Moon and volunteered to cover the least popular time, to everyone's surprise. What they did not realise was that he had believed that it would be the quietest time at the grocery centre since he expected most people to be asleep then, not just the Royals.

King Johannes not only met more citizens than the other Royals, he also met those who had the toughest jobs, the longest hours, and highest work credits—Lunar engineers. Unlike most of the other citizens on Moon, many of the engineers applied for the transfer to Moon to allow them to work with different technologies, equipment that would not have been available or even possible on Earth. When interviewed, most had the same story: normal work hours and decent work credits on Earth, but no opportunities to work with more creative and interesting technologies. On Earth, they had no opportunities to invent or test the boundaries of science.

Since there was quite a large pool of engineers on Earth, they were primarily allocated core work that was necessary for the day-to-day support of the communities. There were only a handful of engineers who were allocated work with the corporations or even Blue Planet because most of the creative and inventive work was given to scientists, whose resource allocations were justified for research and development.

Though Blue Planet was getting better at predicting future skills gaps to create more effective and efficient training for the younger generation, there were still mismatches in skills and jobs due to knowledge trends. No doubt the developments on Moon would encourage a whole new generation to consider Moon-based skills, especially in engineering.

The grocery centre was a large square building, with only four walls and a flat roof. The set-up was very simple, with rows and rows of vegetables and fruits and canned food, clearly laid out for easy packing. There were five counters to the front of the building, where people came to collect their rations. Everyone had to present their ration cards, but as allocations were generous, there were no issues of dishonesty. Families could pick a representative to collect for everyone as long as the representative held all the necessary ration cards.

King Johannes chose to sit on one of the collecting counters to greet citizens, as it provided the best access to everyone coming in. It was during one of the nights when a citizen walked in and caught his attention. The man was skinny, tall and somewhat gawky. He painted the image of a bumbling idiot. Anticipating this man to trip up and embarrass himself, Johannes kept a curious eye on him, and was completely surprised when he saw the man head straight to the far end of the building, where the grocery centre staff were taking their breaks. Johannes was very sure in his judgement that the gangly man could only be an engineer, coming in at that time and looking terribly geeky. He was further bewildered when he saw the man walk toward the exit of the building with a beautiful woman by his side, who had a head full of fiery red hair.

As one who could not control his curiosity, Johannes abandoned his conversation with a citizen who was asking lots of questions about applying to be an engineer with Blue Planet with a wave of his hand. He intercepted the odd-looking couple on their way out.

"Hello, citizens. You must both be just getting off your work shift?"

Greeted with silence, King Johannes realised that his targets were somewhat shy.

"I'm sorry, I haven't introduced myself. I'm Johannes, one of the Royal Committee members. There are four of us on Near Side and we have arranged for a sort of get-to-know-you desk here at the grocery centre for the week." The King stuck out his hand towards the awkward man hoping that he would reciprocate, which he did.

As the men shook hands, the red-haired woman said in a meek voice, "Pleased to meet you, King Johannes. I work here at the grocery centre and I saw you come in when Queen Catherine left earlier." She proceeded to look towards her feet, withdrawing into her husband's shadows, as if she was uncomfortable speaking.

Taking the cue from his wife, the man perked up and added, "Yes, it is an honour to meet you, Sir. I'm Horace and this is my wife, Magdalena."

"Please, please, call me Johannes. Our royal titles are just that now, titles. We are alike, you and I, we are just citizens working for the betterment of our communities."

Horace and Magdalena nodded seriously at King Johannes's statement, agreeing with him and impressed with his humility. Johannes took a moment to allow himself to feel a bit proud, unused to saying aloud what the Royals have nicknamed their first Blue Planet commandment. Confused at his own emotions, King Johannes was somewhat perplexed to find that he actually felt some truth in the statement. He never thought that he would be taking this citizens meeting thing seriously. It had always been in his mind, just a matter of role-play, him as a Royal Committee member, and the citizens as citizens.

"Look, I don't want to take up your time, especially when you're clearly tired from a late shift, but if it's ok, I would like to just find out a little bit about the two of you and how you're finding life to be on Moon."

Magdalena, still hiding in his shadow, gave Horace a gentle tug on his arm.

He looked down at his wife and smiled, before turning to King Johannes. "I came to Moon with my parents. My father has Alzheimer's disease and our Earth community did not really appreciate that mother and I were not pulling our weight. We couldn't, really, since father requires someone with him all the time. I was only working part-time which, as you can imagine, means that our household output was very low."

King Johannes nodded in appreciation, finding that Horace's story was somewhat different from other engineers who had sought out Moon jobs for their novelty value.

There was another perceptible tug from Magdalena and Horace turned to whisper at her.

Turning back to King Johannes, Horace added, "As for Magdalena, her parents kept her sheltered and protected all her life. They even worked more so that she would not need to. She always felt that she led a blessed life, until the day when both her parents died in a transport accident. She did not know what to do, and not wanting to face questions from her community about why she had never worked, she decided that a change in the her life would be helpful."

"And now? Here? How are you two finding it?"

"We're very happy here. Even though father still requires help and attention, the three of us are able to hold down regular jobs and provide for our community properly. Everyone is very understanding with father's situation, even allowing mother to work as a seamstress with her own set-up in our bunker. With the late shifts that Magdalena and I have, it means that we can help watch father when we get back late, whilst mother rests, and in the mornings, we help watch father whilst she works to meet her daily output. It's a good arrangement."

"That's great, and thanks for sharing. Seems everyone on Moon is happy with being here. Oh, and what do you think about living on Moon? I mean, is it as scary as you had thought? Are there any physical discomforts, like the dark and bright periods?"

Magdalena quietly shook her head as Horace replied, "To be honest, we are kept busy enough that we do not think much about our surroundings. We're comfortable, we feel safe and I think I speak for the four of us in our family when I say we're happy."

King Johannes thought that Horace had sounded melancholy, rather than happy, but he put it down to the difficult times they had on Earth. As he thanked them for their time, he asked if they would mind being interviewed later on, perhaps for an official report back to Blue Planet.

Horace shrugged and said, "Sure, why not?" as he shook King Johannes's hand goodbye. Magdalena smiled as she led Horace away from the grocery centre, eager to get back to their bunkers.

Left alone with his own thoughts, King Johannes wanted to speak with someone, but he had foolishly let Thomas take the night off. He felt that Horace and Magdalena had touched a nerve of his with their story. So sincere and so heartbreaking, but yet they said it with no remorse, just acceptance. King Johannes didn't know why, but he just wanted to help them and make their lives better.

Chapter 11

"Wow, Johannes, you're cooking dinner for us?" Queen Silvia exclaimed as she walked into their shared bungalow on Moon. Prince Mohamed and Queen Catherine were sitting in the living area that oversaw the open kitchen where King Johannes was tossing a salad.

"Shush Silvia, don't spoil the moment. We just came down about five minutes ago and we didn't want to say anything in case he changes his mind," Catherine joked, Johannes's new bout of optimism rubbing off on the rest.

"Tease all you want. Since you know how rare it is to taste my cooking, you should be grateful and show your appreciation better," King Johannes said, trying to sound a little more annoyed, but failing. He was adamant about basking in his newfound passion to help. He had, after all invited the other three Royals to have dinner with him that night, so that he might speak to them about Horace and Magdalena's story. Unsure about how he could help them, he was seeking advice from the others, an action that was as foreign to him as it was to anyone who knows him.

"I do apologise on behalf of these two lovely ladies, Johannes," Mohamed said playfully, "and I am sure that they agree with me when I say thank you for this wonderful gesture." Prince Mohamed got up from the couch and walked towards the kitchen where King Johannes was plating the dishes.

"Yes, yes, Mohamed. I'm grateful for your kind thoughts, but I know you're still being sarcastic."

"What are we having for dinner, anyway?"

"A simple meal of steamed fish and vegetables."

"Fish! Now, I haven't had fish since we landed on Moon," Silvia exclaimed, settled on the sofa next to Queen Catherine. "Where did you get that?"

"Oh, just from the grocery centre. You remember Johnny, the supervisor there? He thought that we were doing such a great job of talking to citizens that he wanted us to have a little treat. He even gave me a few tips for tonight's recipe."

"Are you still going back there? We finished our work there weeks ago," Silvia said as she fought her inner instincts to grill Johannes. She was not used to not knowing what every Royal Committee member was doing publicly.

"Only just for this week's grocery collection. I told Thomas, Ronaldo, Sarah and Qamari that I wanted to do it, so they handed me our ration cards. Why, is anything wrong?"

Both Catherine and Mohamed shot Silvia a look, cautioning her not to burst Johannes's bubble. They knew that he was just enjoying the honeymoon period of his community service and that if discouraged, he will probably return to his old ways quicker than they could blink.

"No, no. I just wanted to head back there myself to discuss what else we could do for them. Maybe we could go together, next time?" suggested Queen Silvia, hoping that King Johannes did not see through her attempt to cover-up the fact that she just needed to be in control and in charge.

"Oh, of course. Yes, it'll be good if we went again together." King Johannes handed two plates to Prince Mohamed as they all gathered around the dinner table.

As they were all settling down to dinner, Queen Catherine jumped out of her seat and said, "Two secs," as she ran to her study. Returning immediately after, she had collected the only bottle of wine she had brought with her to Moon, one of the relics in her museum.

"Is that real wine, Cate?"

"Yes, Silvia. I've only ten bottles left—this and nine other bottles on Earth. These were from my family's vineyard before the Great War."

"Wow. It must be worth a fortune," said Prince Mohamed, who was holding the bottle, staring at the label that said *Castellare di Castellina 2004 Chianti Classico Riserva*. His fingers lightly stroked the beautifully painted picture of a red bird. This was a real antique.

"Only in the black market, of course. No one would touch antiques in the open market anymore, especially not wine." As she reached over to take the bottle from Prince Mohamed, she added, "I was told that is a rosefinch, which was quite commonly found back then."

Nodding in appreciation, they stared as Queen Catherine took out a vacuum wine opener from her trouser pocket and placed it over the top of the bottle.

"Are you sure you want to open it, Cate?" King Johannes asked, his eyes glued to the bottle.

"Yes, and stop staring, you all. I brought a bottle with me on this trip as I thought that we would surely have celebratory moments that would call for it. Our success at the grocery centre surely counts for something." Catherine pulled the opener that was holding on to the cork, firmly. As it opened, it let out a satisfying sigh.

"There's also your success with the Coughin machine, Cate," added Prince Mohamed.

Silvia reached out and helped Catherine serve the wine as they all murmured in agreement. Each seeming to have forgotten that they used to drive each other up the wall to no end.

Settled, they all raised their glasses, quietly acknowledging their own achievements so far and each feeling happy being on Moon.

As they enjoyed their dinner, all surprised at Johannes's culinary skills, he told them of Horace and Magdalena's story. He tried to sound neutral and just gave the others facts about the couple's lives as he had heard them, but the others could sense his concern. They were somewhat pleased to finally see the more sensitive side of King Johannes. With their successes fresh in their minds, they wanted to help Johannes, and in turn help Horace and Magdalena.

"What a tragic story."

"Yes, but what can we do to help?"

They brainstormed ideas late into the night but they couldn't come up with anything good. In the end, they decided to invite Horace and Magdalena and the parents over to the bungalow for a private interview, to find out more in hope that they might be able to help them further.

Chapter 12

THERE WAS AN AIR of expectation at the bungalow when the Franks were invited for a private interview with the Royals. Horace's original doubts about King Johannes dissipated with the invitation they received, a chance to meet the other Royals, who were more publicly known for their services to the community.

Since an invitation from the Royal Committee served as official Blue Planet business, it was unnecessary for the Franks to take time off work. Rather, they just had to announce a day out of their regular work routine on community business.

The Franks marvelled at how simple the bungalow was when they arrived, expecting to find more lavish accommodations. The four Royals did not have their assistants with them and were dressed casually, like all other Lunar workers, in plain clothing. It would have been difficult for them to be recognised on the streets if they were not in a group. Four very different characters, they made an odd band, like a twentieth century advertisement for cultural tolerance.

They all sat down to tea and biscuits, or as Queen Catherine called it, "a civilised start," which they had all chuckled over. It helped break the ice for the conversations to flow. King Johannes shed the last of his royalness, openly discussing his sheltered life so far. The others, shocked at such a profound change in him, felt humbled and wondered what it must have been like for him to have experienced such an episode of enlightenment.

Queen Catherine, as it was her habit on Moon, kept an open channel on her private communication device with Sarah so that she was apprised of the situation. Catherine wondered silently if Sarah and the other PAs shared information. What would they be thinking of Johannes's display of empathy and humility? She was sure that his PA, Thomas, would not be supportive, but hoped that she was wrong. Both of their nonchalant characters could have been a facade to cover deeper, darker truths.

Horace's father was in a withdrawn state throughout their visit, but he was docile, happy to adhere to his wife's tugs and quiet suggestions. The Royals could see how the family loved Mr. Frank and paid close attention to his needs, their own needs coming last.

As the cordial discussions faded into more serious talks about what needs the Franks may have, the Royals decided to give them a tour of their bungalow in twos. Queen Catherine and Prince Mohamed would play tour guide to Mr. and Mrs. Frank whilst Queen Silvia and King Johannes would take Horace and Magdalena. They were hoping that with the newlyweds on their own, they would be more willing to discuss their dreams and hopes for the future.

As the first group approached Queen Catherine's study, Mrs. Frank stopped in her tracks when she spotted the Coughin machine.

"Sorry to startle you, that's the Coughin machine," said Queen Catherine.

"Yes, it is one of the newest technologies we have at Blue Planet," added Prince Mohamed.

"It's…it's beautiful," Mrs. Frank managed to stammer a reply before asking, "What does it do? Is it a special bed?"

Chuckling, Prince Mohamed said, "You're not too far off there. It's a machine that is able to collect energy from our brains when we dream. Cate's one of the first people to work with it."

"Dr. Coughin also has twenty volunteers on Earth working with the machines. We're hoping to roll it out for wider usage soon. It's just going through the final stages of checks and approvals."

"Can anyone work with it? Do you have to be healthy, or physically able?"

"Anyone can work with a Coughin machine. In fact, one of the discussions that we are having right now is whether the first phase should be offered to citizens with disabilities, since this would be considered a high-output job."

"You mean, someone like me, or even my husband, with Alzheimer's could work with this Coughin machine?"

"Yes, that's right."

Realising the potential for work with the Coughin machine to better their lives, Prince Mohamed proceeded to ask, "Would this be something that you would consider doing? The both of you?"

"Well…" Mrs. Frank hesitated before asking, "is it safe?"

"Yes, of course. I've been using it for a few months now and most of the power used by our bungalow comes from it. It doesn't hurt at all, and in fact, I sleep better in it," Queen Catherine said as she gently ushered Mr. and Mrs. Frank nearer to the machine.

"Can…uhm…can we try it?"

Queen Catherine laughed gently as she replied, "Not yet, no. You need a small chip implant at the back of your neck to connect to the machine." She told them as she lifted her hair behind her neck to show them the small, slightly protruding implant.

"Does that hurt?"

"It was a painless procedure, and actually, it saved my life."

Prince Mohamed stepped in to explain, "You see, Cate used to get terrible migraines and part of the chip implant is the cure for migraines that Dr. Coughin had discovered."

"That's wonderful," Mrs. Frank said, and as she turned to her husband, she added, "isn't it, love? Would you like to try working with this beautiful machine?"

Mr. Frank turned and in what seemed to be a moment of lucidity, he nodded at his wife and smiled.

"Yes, love. If both you and I can work with these machines, then we can help Horace and Magdalena build a better life for themselves. Maybe they'll even start a family."

Mr. and Mrs. Frank seemed to be having a quiet moment of their own as Prince Mohamed and Queen Catherine looked on. Both Royals knew that they had found a way to help the Franks.

"Mr. Frank, Mrs. Frank, why don't you leave it with us for now. The Royal Committee are due for a meeting to decide on the next steps for the Coughin machines, and I would like to suggest to my colleagues that the both of you could be involved in the next phase, working with the Coughin machines. I'm sure that the activity credits for the work will be more than enough to ensure that the both of you and Horace and Magdalena have comfortable lives."

Nodding, Mrs. Frank reached out to hold Queen Catherine's hand to show her gratitude.

"We have to ask, though. Would you and Mr. Frank mind going back to Earth?" asked Prince Mohamed. "I don't think that we will be considering opening Energy Centres here on Moon, not initially anyway."

"We would be happy anywhere that my husband can get the care he needs, and that we can help Horace and Magdalena in their lives."

"We understand. Look, as soon as the next phase of development takes place, we will come by and speak with you again, probably in about a month's time. Perhaps we could even talk about arrangements for the both of you then."

"That'll be lovely. Thank you."

I remember our visit to the four Royal Committee members' bungalow. We were all excited, even your grandfather. Even though we had heard that the Royals were no longer treated with esteem, we ignored them as rumours as you would think that old habits die hard, right? They were humble and lovely. I don't know why, but King Johannes really wanted to help us.

He seemed sad with his own past. Openly telling us about how he had led a sheltered life amongst royalty. It was as if we were the first normal people that he had met. How crazy is that? I was surprised, as your mother seemed more relaxed too, even joining in conversations with Queen Silvia. I think Magdalena was inspired by Queen Silvia, who is such a powerful figure amongst the Royals.

Your grandparents spent a long time with Queen Catherine and Prince Mohamed. You know I don't agree with idle gossip, but I think they were lovers. They seemed to have the perfect partnership, always gentle and caring towards each other, and respectful too. It's a lovely thing to watch.

They showed us the Coughin machine, which is widely used now, but that was one of the first units. It was amazing and beautiful, though I remember thinking that it looked just like a glass coffin to me. (I've never told anyone that.) Grandmother Frank was enthralled with it. I don't know why as she was never one to enjoy or keep up with new technology. Queen Catherine and Prince Mohamed spent a long time talking with Grandmother and Grandfather Frank when your mother and I had explored the rest of the bungalow.

Magdalena and I were curious about what they talked about, but we never got to find out until a few months later when Queen Catherine and Prince Mohamed came to visit us.

They had arrived just before your mother and I were about

to go to work. I remember Queen Catherine apologising to Grandmother Frank for not visiting sooner and your grandmother shushed her and just said that she had no doubt they would keep their word. Magdalena and I had no idea what was going on.

Queen Catherine and Prince Mohamed told us that the Royal Committee, with approval from citizens, had just started the next phase with the Coughin Machines. They were opening the first Energy Centre in the Blue Planet headquarters so that the first group of citizens can work with the machines. And your grandmother and grandfather were offered positions to work there.

From all the tests that Blue Planet scientists have done, the machines had proven to be 100% safe. It's crazy thinking about it now when there are so many Energy Centres on Earth, but back then, it was a groundbreaking and life-changing discovery for us. They told us that anyone could work with the machines, even Grandfather Frank, with Alzheimer's. In fact, the Blue Planet scientists thought that it might even help with his condition. There was no reason at all why your grandmother couldn't work with the machines.

Except, they would have to leave us and go back to Earth. I knew that this was an opportunity of a lifetime for them, and the best decision as well, but I felt sad. I had lived all my life with my parents, it would be a massive change to not have them around. And we had been so happy—the four of us—as a family in the nine months we were on Moon together.

Your grandparents left for Earth a week later. Your grandmother had told us that she would not write, but Blue Planet assured us that they would contact us with any news from them. We could also email them anytime we liked.

That was seven, nearly eight years ago now. And now, we are all back together again.

A couple of weeks after Mr. and Mrs. Frank were transferred back to Earth, Queen Catherine voiced her doubts to Prince Mohamed, for the first time.

"Mohamed, was it right? What we did for Mr. and Mrs. Frank?"

"Yes, I think so. Why?"

"I can't explain it, but I just feel uncomfortable about something."

"The Coughin machine?"

Queen Catherine nodded as she stood up to walk towards the window in Prince Mohamed's study, glad this once that they weren't in her study where the Coughin machine sat. She fiddled with her necklace out of habit now, as she had already given Sarah access to their conversation as soon as they had sat down for their meeting. Queen Catherine found it comforting to know that Sarah was listening, as they were able to have debriefs every evening about the daily events. Catherine appreciated more and more the comfort of Sarah's feedback. Even the conversation Queen Catherine was having with Prince Mohamed now was proposed by Sarah, who was aware of the doubts that Queen Catherine was having.

"Our scientists have found no ill effects from the Coughin machines, and I think Nemo and Freya are good people and would not hide anything from our scientists, especially not from us."

Nodding, Catherine said, "Yes, I agree completely, but I still don't have a good feeling about it."

"Actually, I have been thinking about getting the chip implant myself, so that I may help on the work with the Coughin machines."

"No, please don't do it."

"Why not?"

"I don't know, Mohamed. I really can't explain it, but I would feel better if you didn't. Please, promise me."

Mohamed could see how distressed Catherine was with this conversation, so he nodded. Trying to help, he added, "Why don't we give it another year before we consider recommending it to anyone else?"

Nodding again, Queen Catherine felt a bit calmer.

"What about you? Do you feel comfortable working with the machine?"

"Yes, of course. My reports so far have been truthful. I think that it is an amazing piece of technology and I'm honoured to be working with it. I only just started feeling apprehensive after we recommended Mr. and Mrs. Frank."

"Perhaps you are concerned because they are elderly, and because of Mr. Frank's condition?"

"Perhaps. But we needn't hurry anything. Another year, ok?"

"Yes, of course. Another year."

Chapter 13

YOUR MOTHER AND I *took our first holiday together a couple of months after your grandparents went back to Earth. We found that we had spare time and we took a day off work. At that time, we both worked the late shifts each day, so we tended to have the mornings to ourselves.*

We also did not have any new bunkmates, even after your grandparents left for Earth. We were lucky, I guess, and we enjoyed having all that space. It was the most beautiful time of our lives, where we spent every morning just talking, the two of us, finding out about things that we had never known of each other, and of ourselves too. We also finally consummated our marriage.

Have you been taught sex education yet? I remember when we were taught that in school. I was only twelve. Many of my friends knew more than I did and many of them lost their virginity only a few years later, whilst I held on to mine until I gave it to your mother, and she, the same. It was beautiful.

But I digress. On the eve of our holiday, I got back to our bunker and told your mother to pack up a small overnight bag with things she might need for a very short trip. She was curious about my plans, but I kept mum, insisting that it should be a surprise. I told her that it was going to be an early anniversary celebration.

We went to the train station and we caught the midnight train out. The trains on Moon aren't very fast, as they have to manoeuvre through difficult terrains and through the glassed atmospheric areas and the non. Anyway, we were on the train for quite a few hours, and we slept for most of the way there.

When we neared our destination, your mother got really excited as she realised that it was the newly completed Earth Sanctuary Resort on Near Side that we were headed to. We entered the glassed atmospheric area that encased the entire resort. It was filled with plants of every sort, colouring the world green, with splashes of bright colours from flowers and fruits. After a year, it was exhilarating to see, and be reminded of the flora that is essential to our home on Earth.

When we got off the train, we both took in deep breaths, nearly choking at the heavy airs. The scents from the plants around us caused many people arriving with us to cough and sneeze. It was quite a funny sight, which we all laughed at. Resort staff were at hand to check every new guest for allergies and to administer antihistamine as necessary. Your mother and I were fine, and after a few minutes we strolled along the walking paths that were lined with flowering bushes and buzzing with imported bees and butterflies. We followed the signs to Relax Relax Hotel.

Do you remember the story of when your mother and I met? How I was completely taken by her beautiful red hair that reminded me of hibiscus? When we arrived at our hotel, I presented your mother with another surprise. I had booked us in an hibiscus themed room.

The room was plainly decorated in pastel colours, which emphasised the hibiscus plants placed all around us. They were all in full bloom, in yellows and reds, and the perfume was intoxicating. I remember looking at your mother as we both took in the space, holding her hand and whispering to her, 'You are my hibiscus', when she looked back at me with tears in her eyes. I was filled with love and joy at that moment, and I am sure that your mother was too.

The porter showed us our simple room, recommending the use of our balcony, which overlooked the main forest of the resort. And before he left us, he handed us two pairs of dark glasses, explaining that there was going to be an eclipse when we were there, and that we should use the glasses if we wanted to see it. We thanked him and settled into our personal sanctuary, our most breathtaking home in our lives, even if it was just for a holiday.

The hotel was the most luxurious experience we have ever had, the perfect honeymoon, even if it was a year late. They brought us meals to our room, made of fresh fruits and vegetables that were grown locally within the resort, and we spent our time there enjoying quiet time together on our room balcony and in walks around the resort.

We read up about the eclipse before it happened. It was a lunar eclipse, if observed from Earth, and a solar eclipse for us, since we were on Near Side. The moon, Earth, and the sun were coming together in a straight line, with Earth in between. We saw photographs of previous eclipses on the hotel's infopad, but nothing prepared us for the actual event.

We sat on deck chairs on the balcony, and watched, as Earth seemed to slowly move in line with the sun. We were bathed in a gentle red glow, as if someone had tinted the air on Moon. The skies were completely clear, creating a never-ending canvas for the occasion. As Earth took its place in front of the sun, everything got redder and redder, until it all blended with the hibiscus around us. When Earth was finally in position, it became a perfect black hole, with a dazzling silhouette, the most beautiful diamond and ruby encrusted ring. That moment made me realise that we, humans, are so insignificant in this world. I was in awe of the power of the sun, realising that even something as simple as looking at the sun directly could harm our eyes, or even blind us. And without the sun, no plants or animals could survive.

Those few minutes also reminded your mother and I of all that we have, and how blessed we were to have found each other. We wanted the moment to last forever, and in some way, I think we managed to do it.

Your mother and I wanted to tell you about that trip, because it is the most important trip of our lives. If you haven't already guessed, you were conceived there, Sun.

When we were on the train back, your mother told me that she was pregnant. I didn't completely believe her then, as I knew that it usually took a few weeks for symptoms to appear, but Magdalena was adamant. I don't know how, but she even knew that you were a girl.

We were both happy and content, knowing that we would be a family soon.

It was another typical evening at the bungalow on Moon for the four Royal Committee members and their assistants. An evening sat around the living room, discussing recent happenings and action plans.

"So, Johannes," Queen Silvia prodded as she helped herself to another cup of coffee that Ronaldo had brewed. "What's your next project now that the Franks are doing better?"

Queen Catherine and Prince Mohamed were sat at the dining table with Qamari and Sarah, going through their notes whilst keeping an ear on the conversation. All four stopped what they were doing and looked up at King Johannes expectantly.

"Franks, huh? Yeah. Did you hear? Magdalena is pregnant."

"That's great news," interjected Queen Catherine.

"Horace and Magdalena must have found some spare time now that his parents have been back on Earth for what, nearly half a year?" said Prince Mohamed with a cheeky smile that spread across the room.

"We should try and follow their progress. Their story will be good for the public reports about Moon," suggested Queen Silvia, always thinking about ways to gain good PR for Blue Planet.

"Yes, of course. I hear that she's nearly three months in, expecting around April," agreed King Johannes.

"You haven't answered my question though. What's your next project?"

"What next project? I'm not done with this project. One project is too many for me anyway."

That last remark earned a snigger from Thomas, King Johannes's PA who was not entirely comfortable with the new sympathetic character that his boss had adopted. Thomas had always been loyal to the cheeky, fun, and guiltless character King Johannes had always been.

"You can't just make one family your project forever, Johannes. It's not fair to the citizens, or to the Franks. They deserve some privacy and freedom."

"Oh, I don't intend to be in their way. I think I'll just be their lucky charm. You know, making sure that they have good luck in their lives from now on. They won't even know that I'm around."

"I don't know what you're planning at, but remember that we have other citizens to think about too."

"No, Silvia, you have other citizens to think about. Cate and Mohamed have other citizens to think about. Thomas and I have done our part for Moon and now it's time to continue our holiday," he finished with a wink to Thomas, who was openly laughing now behind King Johannes who was slouched on the sofa.

Shaking their heads, the other Royals decided to ignore King Johannes for now and continue with their updates, realising that they were probably desperately wrong in thinking that he would ever change.

"Anyway," Queen Silvia addressed the others as she walked to join them at the dining table, "our one year is up next month. Any of you thinking of staying on a little longer?"

"I think another year would be good," suggested Queen Catherine. "What do you think, Mohamed?"

"Yes, another year is realistic. It'll just be to strengthen our ties with the community here."

"That's settled then. I had thought of a year too, so I'll let Mumbaza know. Johannes? You staying?"

"Sure, it's an easier life here. Another year sounds great." He flashed his pearly whites at the group, tempting Queen Catherine to lash out at him as she used to do, but she held her tongue.

Chapter 14

KING MUMBAZA WAS HAPPY to be staring at a roomful of smiling Royal faces. Even the four on Moon seemed content, despite the recent dispute he had heard about King Johannes's idea of community work. Nonetheless, spirits were high with the anticipation of discussions and results on the tender process for Kagami.

With everyone seated and ready, King Mumbaza announced, "I don't want to keep us waiting any longer, so Silvia, if you would like to take the chair of today's meeting."

"Thank you, Mumbaza," Queen Silvia said as she tapped on her tablet to bring the focus of the main camera in the bungalow and all attention to her.

"The public announcements for the results on the tender process for Kagami will be made in two weeks' time. I will be able to let you all know the result now, which is currently only known by the winning organisation and a small Blue Planet team of scientists putting things in place for the big unveiling."

"Sanctuary Holdings, the real estate organisation with a very strong environmental portfolio, won the tender bid by a close margin against EcoBio Ltd. Both had very similar submissions, suggesting 'do not exploit' policies for the new planet. This policy means that all developments on the planet must comply with the strictest environmental guidelines, forever preserving the natural resources as close to as nature had intended."

"It's good to know that our last few years of environmental campaigning have succeeded in getting the information across to citizens," added Queen Silvia with most in the meeting nodding in agreement.

"The two main differences between the two submissions were: 1) EcoBio opened their tender submission to the public and the application came from the idea of one citizen, named Herb Mack, whilst Sanctuary Holdings's tender submission was an internal project for the organisation. And 2) EcoBio suggested the use of Kagami purely as a visiting planet, like a theme park, or a zoo—a place where we could visit and appreciate nature. Their justification for this was that if Kagami were ever open to any human settlements, it would inevitably be polluted, making it impossible to maintain the 'do not exploit' policy. However, Sanctuary Holdings won over the public's votes in this case, because their proposal includes using Kagami as a sanctuary for future generations."

"Who didn't see that coming? Sanctuary wants to create a sanctuary!" King Johannes couldn't help himself as he sat guffawing at his own joke. It was a good thing that he was on Moon, as Queen Silvia was able to switch the attention back to herself.

"Thank you, Johannes," Queen Silvia paused to gather her thoughts. "This sanctuary, or haven, or refuge, whatever you want to call it, will be for the use of our children only. The proposal sets out very detailed and clear guidelines on organisation and access—which you've all been sent a copy of to read in your own time. In general, initially, children from six months up to twelve years are accepted. For every ten children on Kagami, there will only be one adult. The adults will be recruited for specific roles, like teachers, doctors, and nurses. No parents will be allowed to accompany their children and that is non-negotiable."

"As you can imagine, the efforts, manpower and materials needed to put this in action will be quite substantial. In order for Sanctuary to justify the costs involved, the children selected for Kagami must be from a variety of communities and backgrounds. There will be a strict quota for children from families that earn high activity credits, which will allow a quota of children from disadvantaged backgrounds to be considered too. We are currently thinking up job promotions, to tie in current high demand job roles that need filling, with a position for a child on Kagami."

"Zheng is leading this work, so if you have any ideas, or if you are working on recruitment opportunities that could be tied in, please coordinate with Zheng."

Queen Silvia switched the camera view so that the Boardroom saw Emperor Zheng's face instead. He nodded lightly and added, "As Silvia mentioned earlier, information and some initial ideas are included in the pack. Ming Li is helping me coordinate," he said gesturing at his assistant.

In his usual abrupt way, Emperor Zheng slouched back in his chair without another word. King Mumbaza, used to his mannerisms, stepped in.

"Any questions for Silvia or Zheng at this point?"

Queen Sia was the first to raise her hand with a question. "Silvia, I understand that the children who will be sent to Kagami will not be able to have their parents with them, and that this is non-negotiable."

Queen Silvia looked into the camera and nodded clearly for the benefit of those on Earth.

"How is this news received by citizens? I am surprised that they had voted for this tender application with such a harsh requirement."

"Actually, I can help answer that," said King Mumbaza as Silvia nodded. "I have spoken to community leaders about the votes, and when we discussed this tender submission and the point of separating the parents from the children, it seems that most parents today don't get to see their children much anyway. From six months, babies are left with community nurseries that in the last half a year have started looking after the babies and children full-time. Parents visit their children at the nursery when it suits and bring them out on rest days, but ultimately, the children have started living at the nurseries."

"Really? Why haven't we heard about this earlier?" Queen Sia was clearly perturbed by the news.

"Well, changes like these are made within communities and do not need the approval of anyone else, as you know—least of all from us. It seems one of the nurseries started the programme to cater for parents with long work hours, it became twenty-four hours, and it caught on with surrounding communities."

"So, this is recent?"

"Yes, sometime in the last six months."

"I still find it surprising that parents would part with their children. But perhaps community nurturing rather than nucleic family nurturing is the way forward."

"Yes. And perhaps we on Earth need to take a leaf out of our four Moon colleagues' book and pay more direct attention to our community," suggested King Mumbaza, hoping that he did not come across as haughty. "Anyway, are there anymore questions before we go off and read and absorb all the information we were given?"

Tired and seemingly defeated, most of the Royal Committee members sat staring at the documentation that were laid out in front of them.

"Remember, people, read up, do your homework and think up promotion possibilities." Queen Silvia beamed at everyone, somehow forcing some energy to the rest. Most of them smiled back in return.

"Yes, thank you everyone," King Mumbaza added as the video link between Moon and Earth was ended.

"Phew," breathed Queen Silvia, "that was weird."

"What happened? It was supposed to be a positive meeting, with the announcement of the winning submission." Queen Catherine said, quietly aware that it was inevitable for Queen Silvia to ask her about promotional possibilities in recruiting potential parents who would like to have their children on Kagami, since they could easily offer work with Coughin machines in exchange.

"I guess we are all just nervous about whether it's the right decision."

"The tender winner? That's not our choice…we shouldn't be nervous about it. The people choose, the people get," said King Johannes matter-of-factly.

"Johannes is right," agreed Prince Mohamed.

"Anyway, Cate, do you want to lead the discussions about promoting Coughin machine work alongside children's acceptance to Kagami?"

Before Catherine could reply, Mohamed cut in, suggesting, "Wouldn't it be better if Nemo's office handled that directly? It would probably be more assuring to the parents interested. And Cate and I can help with questions, support and PR where needed."

"That does make more sense. Mohamed, could you speak with Nemo to see if he could appoint someone at his office, maybe Freya, to speak with Zheng and get the ball rolling?"

"Of course. I think it'll work out well."

Chapter 15

The street lights were still switched on, a sign that citizens on Moon have taken to relying on to tell the time of the day during dark periods. It was early in the evening and many had gone home or to the canteen for dinner. Horace and Magdalena were sat in the kitchen of their bunker with King Johannes, who made a surprise visit alone. Out of courtesy, they had offered him to share some of their dinner and were surprised when he agreed.

King Johannes seemed at home in their kitchen, seemingly unperturbed that they were busy scraping together whatever they had in their larder to feed three, instead of two. They would need to go to the grocery centre later that night.

Magdalena's bump was showing very clearly now that she was in her final trimester. King Johannes did not know much about pregnancies but he could tell that she was nearly ready.

"When are you expecting?"

"Oh," Magdalena gasped in a small voice, as if she was testing her vocal chords. "In two weeks."

"Though the doctor says that the baby might arrive early since Magda is pretty big for this stage of the pregnancy. The baby is ready." Horace said as he served up three bowls of vegetable soup while Magdalena prepared some vegetables and rice.

They all sat around the table to start on the soup.

"Have you thought of a name?" King Johannes started on the soup, not waiting for the others.

"Yes, we are going to name her Sun."

Spattering his soup everywhere, not even trying to hide his amusement, King Johannes laughed out at the suggestion. "You're not joking?" he asked.

Both Horace and Magdalena remained indifferent to King Johannes's outburst. They merely smiled politely as they shook their heads.

"The sun brings us warmth and gives us hope," whispered Magdalena.

"Yes, it is a good name. She will be a strong person who will be able to bring hope and comfort to the people around her, someday."

"Ok, ok. I can see how it's a good name," King Johannes conceded as he continued slurping his soup, having wiped up the mess he had created with his towel. "And do you want Sun to grow up on Moon, or on Earth?" asked King Johannes, trying to tease out their feelings, holding back another outburst of laughter at the absurdity of the name.

"Moon is fine. There are lots of great nurseries here."

"Yes, indeed. But haven't you two thought about the best possible option for Sun? I hear that parents are big on providing the best for their children? No?"

Magdalena got up to serve up the rice and vegetables, looking somewhat uncomfortable with their guest who was oblivious to anyone else's feelings.

"Of course, but we are realistic too. We want the best for Sun that we can provide," Horace responded for the both of them.

There was a pause as they started on their main course. King Johannes shovelled rice into his mouth, buying time, to think about his next approach.

"Have you read the news about Kagami?"

The question seemed to have hit a nerve as both Horace and Magdalena stopped eating and placed their spoons on the table.

Taking his cue, King Johannes continued, "It's a great opportunity for any child to grow up in the perfect environment with the best teachers and doctors around..." He did not end his sentence, allowing the unspoken thoughts to seep naturally into their brains.

Still not eating, Horace reached out to hold Magdalena's hand as he spoke, "Yes, we've read the news and it is incredible. There will be a lot of very lucky children."

"Not Sun? Are you not thinking of applying for Sun?"

"Why apply when we know we will be rejected?"

"What makes you think you'll be rejected?"

"We...we don't earn enough activity credits. And we're not in any special circumstances that would justify lowered activity credits."

"Ah...then you have not heard."

"About what?"

Even King Johannes had stopped eating, enjoying having the upper hand in the conversation. "There are promotional campaigns around the application to enter a child into Kagami. One of them links up working with Coughin machines, like your parents are doing."

"Coughin machines work? Like my parents? What are you talking about?"

"That's why I wanted to come and see you. I wanted you to be the first to know that you can get Sun on Kagami if the both of you transferred to work with the Coughin machines."

"On Earth?"

"Yes, on the same site as your parents, actually. They've moved into the next phase now and we have quite a few Energy Centres, or some call them Coughin Centres on Earth now, ready to recruit at least a thousand new workers to start with."

Magdalena gripped Horace's hand so tight that her knuckles were white.

“This is…is a lot for us to take in. It is an amazing opportunity…but we need time to consider it, and to discuss between us.”

“Of course, of course,” King Johannes said as he picked up his spoon and proceeded to inhale the rest of the food on his plate.

Feeling awkward, Horace and Magdalena tried to eat too, but ended up just moving their rice around their plates.

“Look,” King Johannes stood up as he had finished. “Think about it. The publicity will be distributed in two days’ time, and after that, I can’t promise you places and you’ll have to apply like everyone else. If you make a decision before then, or if you have any questions, you know where to find us.”

Horace and Magdalena stood to see their guest out, but before they could offer him their hands, he had turned to walk out of the door.

Our dearest Sun, the biggest decision your mother and I had to make in our lives, was entering you into Kagami. We were offered an amazing opportunity but it came with a huge sacrifice. You already know what that sacrifice was. Oh, how we long to have you in our arms. How we have missed you.

After we heard about the opportunity, we discussed it through the night, weighing up the good and bad points. We asked King Johannes and Queen Silvia so many questions that we thought they would ask us to withdraw our application. But no matter what we did, the list of good points just grew bigger and bigger, with just one item on the bad—not being there for you when you grew up. In the end, we concluded that our worry of missing out on your childhood years was a selfish one. It was something that your mother and I yearned for, but it was not practical. We knew that if you grew up on Kagami, you’d have the best opportunities available, so that you could grow up to be successful, strong, healthy, and most importantly, happy.

We were glad that we could spend more time with your grandparents too, after we started working with the Coughin machines. Your family is together here, ready to welcome you into our arms when you're ready, when you've gotten the best upbringing and education.

There are days when we wonder if we had made a bad decision, putting you on Kagami whilst we're all on Earth. But we know that we are being silly. How can we ever think that we could do a better job in bringing you up ourselves?

We love you very much, Sun. Don't ever forget that.

Chapter 16

Queen Catherine scrambled from her bedroom to her study in the darkness. She stared at her bedside clock that blinked 03:21 in red. She remembered when she used to sit in the dark, nursing migraines, when she found solace in the dark that seemed so inconvenient now.

She reached for her necklace, holding down the button, feeling guilty for waking Sarah. As she moved along, using her left hand on the wall as a guide, she put in her earpiece with her right hand and waited for Sarah's response.

She heard a click first and a delay of a few seconds, before Sarah's voice came on.

"Cate? What's the matter?"

"Sorry, Sarah. I've been called by Mumbaza who sounded frantic. I'm just going to video call him now, but I wanted you to listen in. We might need to meet after."

"Of course. I'm up now and ready."

"Don't wake the others. Mumbaza was adamant about this being a private call, just between the two of us."

"I understand."

"I trust you, Sarah, but I have no idea what's going on, so it could be big, or it could be nothing."

"Don't worry, Cate. I know."

The conversation ended when Queen Catherine reached her study and switched on her computer to start-up the video link. Feeling nervous, she dialled King Mumbaza's personal line.

The screen changed to show a dishevelled looking King Mumbaza, unshaved and unkempt. He seemed to have put on weight since their last meeting, which was only a few months before.

"What's wrong, Mumbaza?" Queen Catherine whispered harshly, not wanting to wake anyone, but unable to contain her shock.

"Cate. There's more news from the Okinawa guys."

"The scientists? Those who had discovered Kagami?"

King Mumbaza nodded, unable to speak.

"What is it, Mumbaza?"

"They told me and Silvia, a month ago, but I think everyone needs to know."

"Silvia? What is it that you can't tell us? Come on, Mumbaza. This call is confidential, you can trust me."

Nodding, he said, "I know, Cate. I know." Taking a deep breath, he worked up courage to continue. "As they were scanning the vicinity of Kagami, doing their usual checks, they picked up on a signal coming off Kagami. Initially, they thought that it was a stray signal from Earth."

Queen Catherine waited patiently as King Mumbaza stopped for breath, raking his hands through his hair.

"They investigated the signal and followed its path. It led from Kagami, but it wasn't going towards Earth."

"Where did the signal go?" Queen Catherine tried to encourage the conversation on.

"There seems to be some kind of a space craft just outside Kagami's atmosphere."

"Space craft? What do you mean? Something that one of the Directors sent without Blue Planet's consent?"

King Mumbaza shook his head.

"Old NASA space junk?"

King Mumbaza shook his head again.

"Mumbaza, please, just tell me. What is it?"

"That's the thing, Cate. We can't identify it. None of the scientists can."

"What? It's definitely not ours?"

"The technology is different. The external material is...different. That was why we never knew it was there. It seemed like an asteroid, organic matter floating in space. Nothing worth a second look."

"How do we know it's not an asteroid?"

"The signal. It's all because of the signal. The scientists followed the signal from Kagami to this object, and from there, they spotted another signal. It was from Earth to this object."

"What does the signal do? Tell me, Mumbaza." Queen Catherine was getting desperate now and her voice demanding attention.

"The scientists are still trying to decipher the message, but the current belief is that it's data packets. This object is downloading information from Earth. The signal from Kagami must be new as it was only a month ago when we started installing communications on Kagami."

"Mumbaza, please don't joke around. Are you leading me to believe that there's an alien space craft parked outside Kagami eavesdropping on us?"

"Yes, Cate," was all King Mumbaza could manage as he fell to the floor clutching his chest.

s̄un

15 years later

chapter 17

HELLO. MY NAME IS Sun. *I have my mother's red hair and my father's green eyes, but I have never met either of them.*

That was such a stupid introduction, even in my head. Stupid as it was, I never got to use it, not after what had happened, anyway.

Her name is Maaike and she had arrived as a fifteen year old. We were all surprised as we had not had any new students in our class, ever, but we heard that there were changes made to the Sanctuary Rules, allowing older recruits.

For the first few months after her arrival, I had found it very distracting as she used to sit across the hall from me. I stopped listening in class, and I stopped doing any work. I just stared and stared at her. I couldn't stop staring. I had wondered if she realised that I was staring at her and I guess I had my answer since she came over to talk to me on that one fateful day.

For years after Maaike and I became friends, I would forget or pretend to forget about what had happened that day. It was very embarrassing for me, as a teenager back then, but I guess you learn to prioritise things in your life as an adult.

I remember as clearly as if it was yesterday, Maaike had walked over to my desk and when I realised she was coming to talk to me, and not anyone else, I froze. My palms got sweaty and my heartbeat went wild. And when she had approached my desk, my memory told me that I had fainted. I don't think she even had a chance to say anything to me, before I fainted.

I remember waking up in the nurse's office to see Nurse Janice's wrinkly face peering at me, with a smile as wide as her face. She said, "Ah, Sun, you're awake. Guess what? Your period is finally here. You're a woman now, congratulations!"

I had cringed at her. We were taught to be open and frank about our sexuality and bodily functions, and actually, all my friends were quite brazen. I never felt comfortable with the subject, probably because I was what they had called a 'late bloomer'. I thought I had escaped the torment of discussing my body developments after all the other girls in my class got their periods when we were twelve, but it all came back that year; they started pairing us in couples of boy and girl. That was the same year that I had met Maaike and got my period. I was fifteen.

Blue Planet had changed its legislation then, making it compulsory for everyone to have at least one child. We were only fifteen when the teachers had to explain it to us. Populations were dwindling further due to increased comforts in our lifestyle—a consequence of the discovery of the Coughin machines.

We were told that on Earth, everyone slept in Coughin machines. They were used to power everything on Earth, from housebots to generators, to factories. People were able to work whilst doing nothing, whilst machines did all the work that humans used to do.

My grandparents and parents were pioneers in working with the Coughin machines. For most of us who grew up on Kagami, our parents took up the Blue Planet promotion—a space on Kagami for their children, paid for by a lifetime's work with Coughin machines. On Kagami, we had never seen a Coughin machine, other than in pictures and videos. We knew of what it was, and its history, of course, but somehow it was not allowed on Kagami even though all the energy that we used came from Coughin centres.

At fifteen, we found out that there was a crisis on Earth as the population was reducing and getting lazier. Obesity and sicknesses were becoming a problem again (we had learnt in class that both were problems in history, when the separated country nations went through different prosperity periods) with most people doing no physical work, yet justifying it with the high energy output they had with the Coughin machines. Citizens pressured Blue Planet to concentrate on medical sciences and assistance technology so that better medicines could be found to help control the weakening species and more machines could be designed to help with the physical chores.

Queen Catherine nodded to Sarah as they approached the darkest corner of the carpark in the basement of Blue Planet's headquarters. She reached out for her necklace, seeming to be fiddling anxiously with it. She had actually turned on her communicator, allowing Sarah to listen in and record whatever that was going to be taking place. This device, insignificant as it may seem, had helped them keep alive to this day.

Sarah stayed in the car, in the driver's seat, with the engine running.

"Mumbaza," Queen Catherine whispered roughly as she entered the darkened room.

"Cate, it's ok," said Mumbaza, switching on the lights to reveal a humble apartment. Though unshaven and skinny, Mumbaza looked in good spirits.

"You have to stop sitting in the dark," Queen Catherine scolded endearingly as she moved around the kitchen to make herself a cup of coffee. Both Cate and Mumbaza had more lines on their faces and clear greys in their hair.

"Sorry," Mumbaza smirked. "I didn't want to use too much electricity. Don't want to draw attention to my little apartment."

"Look, we've been through this many times. All the energy used in this apartment is from that," she said nodding towards a Coughin machine stored in the corner of the room—her Coughin machine. "No one will be able to detect any energy usage here. Your communications are rerouted too, so any signals coming from here will seem to be coming from China."

"I know, I know. I'm just…worried."

Queen Catherine reached to hold Mumbaza's hand and squeezed it reassuringly. They took a quiet moment to smile before Catherine went over to the Coughin machine, reading the data off the control panel. "You still have a week's worth of energy, so I won't top it up today, ok?"

"Of course. I'll try and live normally, Cate. I promise."

Smiling, she said, "We'll protect you, Baz. You know that, right? Look, I'll bring Mohamed in a couple of days. That way I can top up your stored energy comfortably with Mohamed monitoring and you boys can plan our next moves. Ok?"

"That'll be nice."

They sat in silence for a moment before Mumbaza plucked up the courage to ask Queen Catherine about the goings-on. It was a routine for her visits, so she knew to expect it.

"How is Sisi doing?"

"He's very well. Citizens have even taken to referring to him as King Sisi." That was news to Mumbaza, who had not seen or heard from his ex-assistant in fifteen years. After the heart attack Mumbaza had whilst video conferencing with Queen Catherine all those years ago, the world had thought that King Mumbaza had died. Officially, he was dead. Sisi's quick thinking, with Catherine, Mohamed and Sarah's help, saved Mumbaza from what would have been a worse fate. The only evidence they had of everything that has happened since are the archived recordings from Catherine and Sarah's communicators.

"King Sisi, huh?" Mumbaza smiled inwardly, amused that he was bloated with pride, like an approving father. "It suits him."

Nodding, Queen Catherine added, "You've trained him well. He is just like you…and more, if I dare say. Humble and kind, and yet strong and strict when it comes to dealing with us Royal idiots. He always asks after you when he can, you know."

Holding back his emotions, Mumbaza sat staring into space.

"He knows that it's safer for him if he doesn't know where you are, but he misses you. Sometimes, I think it's no different from grieving."

"Next time, please tell him that I am grieving too, but I am proud of everything that he has done, and grateful too. He is like a son to me."

"I will, and I am sure he knows." She stood up, annoyed that she had to leave on such a low note again.

"Oh, Cate."

"Yeah?"

"Next time, bring me a game or some entertainment, ok?"

"Sure, what would you like?" Queen Catherine was glad for the distraction.

"No more crosswords or Sudokus please. Maybe a tablet with some button bashing games, you know, shooting bad guys or something mindless like that."

Queen Catherine smiled at the thought of Mumbaza playing shooting games, an image that tickled her, as she nodded.

Mumbaza was smiling too as he walked her to the door. They hugged goodbye, and each time they couldn't help but feel that it might be the last time they would see each other.

Chapter 18

As the skies shone with streaks of pink sunset cutting across the old metropolis of skyscrapers, four figures were seen entering the towering glass building that was Blue Planet's headquarters. Though it was odd for anyone to enter the building at that hour, no one bothered Queen Catherine, Prince Mohamed, Sarah and Qamari as they tapped their building passes to access the lifts. They rode in silence up to the Blue Planet offices, going past floor after floor of Coughin Centres, all filled with working citizens lying in the machines.

Arriving on their designated floor, they moved purposefully across the hall, into a smaller meeting room to the right, though Sarah and Qamari did not follow. Instead, they walked in the opposite direction, toward what used to be a server room but was now an abandoned site.

In the meeting room, Mohamed and Catherine moved to take their places, the only two seats that were not filled. The rest held the other eighteen members of The Council, some familiar faces and some surprising ones. Queen Sia stood in the front of the room, not hiding her annoyance that Mohamed and Catherine were part of the group. This was only the fourth meeting that they were invited to attend.

Sia switched off the main lights in the room and the room fell into complete silence, as if the lights had controlled their speech too.

"Need I remind all of you that these proceedings, like all of the others, are not be recorded or discussed outside of these walls?"

There were low murmurs and grunts throughout the room as Catherine fought the urge to touch her necklace, knowing that Sarah and Qamari are both listening in right now.

"Other than Mohamed and Cate, all of you have been selected for your expertise, to help with the situation that we have at hand."

Prince Mohamed reached for Queen Catherine's hand under the table to squeeze it reassuringly. They both knew that this was Queen Sia's way of undermining them in front of the rest of The Council, a punishment for threatening their way into The Council.

Cate and Mohamed had approached Queen Silvia a week after King Mumbaza's collapse, to inform her that they knew of the truth. They pushed Silvia for more information, pleading to her that the Royal Committee needed to go public with the information, that citizens had the right to know. They fought and argued for nearly half a year, before they realised that Silvia was not the one controlling the situation. There wasn't only one person in charge; it was an entire committee—The Council.

After the four Royals moved back to Earth from Moon, Mohamed and Cate pushed Silvia even harder, letting on that they have recorded proof of the information that they would not hesitate to leak out to the public if they were not given access. Reluctantly, Silvia and Sia arranged for Cate and Mohamed to face The Council. That was their first meeting, nearly fourteen years before, which was also their initiation. Now they too were sworn to secrecy.

"There is still no change on the position of the unidentified spacecraft. Their data connections with Earth and Kagami and Moon are still live. The data transfer rates on the connections are very low now, as we've come to realise that they have downloaded all electronic data that is available in human history. Any data movements now are only updates or new data. Brend is monitoring the connection with Moon specifically, as we have created a separate communication channel, for military usage only, which should be hidden from the spacecraft." The recruitment of Thor Hammond and Brend Zoid into The Council was strategic in securing Moon as a classified military base. The Council created a plan after its early gatherings to publicly announce that the Lunar Resort was a failed development. Keeping only a selected number of engineers there on a covert arrangement, all the others who were working on Moon were shipped back to Earth to work with Coughin machines. Since then, Moon became the base for all those researching and working on new technology under the guise of Virgin Red Bull and Cyberity, but truly for The Council. All who worked on Moon are cut off in communications from Earth, or Kagami. The physical barrier of being on Moon seemed the best vantage for the secrecy that The Council needed.

"Since our last gathering four years ago, we have been able to develop new methods to scan objects in space. We can confirm that it is an artificial construct, not a natural satellite. The only conclusion that brings us to is that it is definitely a spacecraft, even if we cannot determine its origin. I'm sure we've all seen the report that Thor and Benjamin put together, covering how the scans were made and the detailed findings of the structure and composition, as far as we can interpret them."

"Sia," interrupted Dr. Benjamin Mitchell, a scientist renowned for his vast multidisciplinary knowledge of the sciences. "I just wanted to add that we have also recently sent a probe to Astro—sorry, I meant the spacecraft," he paused, chuckling at himself. "You see, I nicknamed it Asteroid, as it is very much like one. The probe we sent managed to collect a small material sample from its outer layer, and it is just like what you would expect from a piece of space rock. Some ice, rock, carbon, and nickel-iron. Nothing special, which makes it a great camouflage."

"But, couldn't it be natural? Couldn't it be an asteroid?" asked Catherine, knowing that she was the only one in The Council who still did not believe. Even Mohamed had accepted the fact that the spacecraft was not natural, nor of a human construct.

"Actually Cate, if it was an asteroid, it would be travelling at great speed, especially since it is situated so closely to our planets. The various gravitational forces around it, the pull from our planets' orbits would have moved it, and its size would have decreased from general wear and tear too," explained Ben, not noticing the roll of Sia's eyes at the question. "What I mean is that Astro is actually parked on the spot, which is impossible for any asteroid to do."

Nodding, Catherine knew that she had to accept the fact now.

"And what about life forms?" asked Prince Mohamed, asking the question that no one dared think about.

"We haven't found anything yet," Sia replied, knowing that it was the biggest concern in everyone's minds. "Per the reports, all scans just show the structural design of the spacecraft—I guess we might as well call it Astro, for a lack of a better name. There seem to be catacombs throughout the interior, but there were no heat signatures or movements of any kind."

"Not anything that our technology could pick up, anyway," Thor added, making Sia uncomfortable as to where the discussion might be headed.

"Yes, yes. Thor and I have had many a discussion on this topic—our friends in the Astro. The catacombs suggest that they burrow. The material and structure suggest that they have advanced knowledge in manipulating organic matter. I would make a guess, an educated guess, that they are sentient,"

Benjamin casually remarked, ignorant to the tension in the room.

"The people need to know," Catherine whispered harshly, not intending for the rest to hear, but it was too late.

"Cate, please. The Council, that is you, me, and everyone else in this room, knows that when we feel that we have enough information to give to citizens, we will do it immediately. But in the meantime, we are agreed that we need to research, find out more, and make preparations for whatever outcome."

It was obvious that the rest of The Council agreed on the matter, with only Mohamed unsure now. Cate knew that soon Mohamed would also be convinced that this secret was necessary. There was also Sisi. King Sisi, who wasn't present at this meeting, was on a citizen's function representing the Royal Committee. Catherine hoped that she still had Sisi on her side.

Chapter 19

It was five hours before The Council adjourned from their meeting. No one knew when they would meet together again. Perhaps in a few years, perhaps earlier, but they had their means of communicating and there was work to do for all of them.

It was agreed that military developments should take precedence now that they were sure that they were dealing with a spacecraft, even if there was a lack of life forms on board. They were going to have to prepare for all eventualities. Up until then, The Council had concentrated on using the military space on Moon purely for research and monitoring of Astro, with minimal personnel on site. However, The Council had decided that it was time for military recruitment to begin, and the first target would be the young men on Kagami.

Blue Planet had been having problems considering careers and places in communities for the teenagers and children who were raised on Kagami. The Sanctuary paper had stated how Kagami should be used, but made no mention about what should happen to those who grew up there. The parents of those children were keen to be reunited as families again, but it would mean that the children would also need to consider working with the Coughin machines or at least living in the same community. With machines assisting with most chores and physical work, the demand was in science and research, to help keep sicknesses at bay, and to keep developing new technologies that would help automate even more labour. Citizens were not keen on allowing any humans do the jobs that technology could do for them, even if scientists told them that it was slowly killing humanity through inactivity.

Most, if not all, of the children on Kagami that had reached sixteen years of age were going to be placed in a science or research role on Earth. And it was under the guise of Cyberity and Virgin Red Bull that they would also be placed on Moon for similar roles. However, on Moon, they would also be clandestinely trained for military purposes.

The Council, as well as the rest of the Royal Committee, realised that the issue of a dwindling human population was the priority. It was the only issue that they were all working on publicly. The compulsory minimum one-child mandate was only passed by the Royal Committee five years earlier, and finally approved through global voting for immediate application a year later. Since then, the number of new births had kept scientists in a more positive outlook even though the total population was less than 0.1% of the population pre-Great War.

I watched Maaike give birth when I was four months pregnant myself. It was horrendous and beautiful all at the same time. The father of her child, Anuar, stood by her as he had supported her throughout her pregnancy, but no matter how much warning they had given us beforehand, he was clearly badly affected by it.

I remember thinking that we had never seen that much blood spilled in our lives. Even the worst accident that happened in class was minor in comparison. Lulu had accidentally cut her finger with a new pair of scissors, and the cut was deep, but it had only bled a little. If we had watched a birth on video with friends, it would not have been any different from watching the gory horror films we were shown in media history.

Maaike was given an epidural so she wouldn't feel most of the pain. By then, she had already experienced a few hours of periodical contractions, each worse than before. She kept a brave face, but Anuar and I could see the pain coming through. The doctor and midwife kept telling us that she was *doing very well*, but we were horrified at how much pain doing very well meant. As much as we tried to help Anuar, he was never able to love his child fully. He had loved Maaike too much to be able to see Izanagi, his baby boy, as anything more than a parasite—a monster that latched on to Maaike and destroyed her body.

My own experience was similar, though I had the benefit of having seen Maaike go through it first. I only had Henry, the father of my baby, with me on that day. My contractions had lasted two whole days before I was told that our baby girl, Yhi, was ready to come and face the world. No matter how much pain I experienced, when Yhi arrived, I knew that I wouldn't be able to love anyone else the way I did her. She was precious, beautiful, and mine.

Henry loved Yhi and cared for her like the nurses had taught him. Yhi spent the first few months of her life either in my arms or in Henry's. Maaike and I had also developed a makeshift team then, to take care of the two little ones. Yhi and Izanagi were together from the day Yhi was born.

Before our babies turned one, we were told that Henry and Anuar were going to be transferred to Moon. We were all seventeen then and just waiting to hear about our own assignments. Some of our friends had already been sent to Moon, or back to Earth where they apprenticed with various scientists and engineers. But only the boys were given assignments. Most of us girls were either pregnant or looking after an infant.

Henry and Anuar were very happy to have been assigned together. They had been best friends since forever. Henry found it difficult leaving Yhi. We knew that it was unlikely that they would get to see their babies again. We knew that it was also very likely that our babies would grow up on Kagami, like we did, whilst we were all assigned to Moon or Earth.

Anuar felt relieved, not having to try or pretend to be fatherly anymore. We knew how difficult it was for him, but we were all proud that he tried really hard. But Anuar was stricken about leaving Maaike. It was never Blue Planet's intention to pair us for life—it was always so we could have babies to support humanity's population—but they had fallen in love. When Maaike arrived on Kagami, it was Anuar who greeted her first and they had always been close ever since.

The boys left us two days after they were told of their assignment, with a new uniform on their backs and a small travel pack provided by Cyberity and Virgin Red Bull. They looked like the mountaineers in our history books. There were ten boys in total going to Moon and we were all very excited about them travelling on a space shuttle. We had learnt about the history and how the shuttles worked, but none of us who were brought up on Kagami had ever travelled anywhere before. Except for Maaike, of course, she had travelled from Earth to Kagami when she was older.

Because there were ten boys leaving, we made banners and flags and brought them to the airport. We tried to be happy as we cheered the boys on their journey. As Maaike and I said our goodbyes to Henry and Anuar, none of us promised to write or to keep in touch. I guess we knew that this was the end of a phase of our lives and that we wouldn't ever be together again in the future.

Without Henry and Anuar, Maaike and I became both father and mother for Iz and Yhi. We worried about the day when we would be taken away from Iz and Yhi, and so we strived to make our time together count, hoping that we were making happy memories in our babies' minds. Maaike and I became closer than ever.

We stayed that way until our babies were two years old; watching more boys leave, most of them assigned to Moon, as we helped out with the younger students, guiding and teaching. We felt happy and fulfilled, loving the fact that we had a purpose on Kagami in caring for the younger generation.

That was until we were moved to Earth.

chapter 20

Queen Catherine and Prince Mohamed sat in Mumbaza's secret apartment, sharing notes and thoughts as Qamari and Sarah were working from their car, parked in the carpark just outside.

Sat around the kitchen table, Cate was showing Mohamed and Mumbaza the latest reports from Sia. The military developments were going well, and Cate was feeling uneasy.

"The figures show that there are now over a hundred young men being trained to use the new weapons that they've been working on," said Mohamed as he read the data displayed.

"The Laser Bombs?" asked Mumbaza, using the nickname that the newly designed weapon had earned for itself. An invention born on Moon from the collaboration between Cyberity and Virgin Red Bull's best engineers, the PGCs or Pulse Generating Canons were an ingenious use of the optical amplification process with a breakthrough in pulse control. Basically, large balls of energy in the form of electromagnetic radiation are released in controlled bursts, with the timing and scale of the explosion controllable, making it the most accurate destruction tool around.

They had already been using it in mines and for clearing new construction areas. Though usage had been limited to a small scale, the maximum potential of the Laser Bombs was unimaginable, easily devastating an entire satellite, even one the size of Moon. In fact, it was the perfect weapon to destroy the spacecraft Astro that they all could not figure out.

"Yes. The small Laser Bombs are pretty easy to use, but they are training five men to understand the complex science and technology behind it as they are going to start building a large unit." Mohamed explained, as he continued scrolling through the document on the tablet.

"How large?" asked Cate, as she started to get more anxious.

"It will be approximately three hundred times the size of the ones in usage."

"But, that is impossible!" exclaimed Mumbaza, aware of how much power something that size would require.

"The science isn't impossible. You know that, Baz."

Nodding, Mumbaza explained, "Yes, yes. But the size of the unit would be humungous, like a skyscraper, and the amount of power required would be tremendous."

"That big?" asked Cate, the only one in the room with little knowledge or understanding of how the Pulse Generating Canons worked.

"Yes. And because of the power problem, this report states that the unit will be built in close proximity to the power source."

"But where would that..."

Mumbaza left his sentence hanging as the rest of the room came to the same conclusion, realising that the large unit will be built on Earth.

Mohamed read directly from the report then, "The structure will be erected next to the Blue Planet Headquarters. Direct cabling will run from the Power Storage to the unit. A full Power Storage will not suffice in creating one pulse from the unit. Two additional Power Storages will be built within the structure and cabling from BPH's live sources would be required."

Scrolling further through the document, Mohamed continued, "Construction will take approximately 36 months, with both manual labourers and robotic equipment." Mohamed could see that both Mumbaza and Cate were concerned, and before they could speak, he held up his hand to motion for them to listen a bit more. "The end of the report says that the decision on the construction of the Laser Bomb will be made at the next meeting. The Council is being called together next week."

The three continued to work, creating a plan for the next week. The Council reports were always copied onto small flash drives and personally delivered by a member to the rest. Cate and Mohamed had received theirs earlier that day in their own offices, when Thor had driven around. The Council members tend to base themselves near Blue Planet's headquarters to ensure that news would be received quickly.

The three agreed that the development of the large Laser Bomb must not happen without the knowledge of citizens. The secret of the spacecraft had been held for longer than any of them could accept, but the longer the delay, the more difficult it was to justify informing the public. They knew that this would be the last opportunity for them to insist that the news go public. They were also aware of how secretive The Council was with this knowledge, with most of them believing that information given to an uneducated public would mean chaos.

Though Mohamed would sometimes agree that public consensus was not always the right course of action, Cate and Mumbaza were adamant in upholding the constituency that Blue Planet was created on.

The three of them hatched a plan to go public with the last set of information they had received from The Council should the voting go unfavourably. Sarah and Qamari would wait with Mumbaza at his apartment for Cate and Mohamed's news.

There they would rig up an anonymous connection to the public information system from Blue Planet's communications, releasing the information to Earth, Moon and Kagami simultaneously. It seemed extreme, but they were all sure that it was the right thing to do.

Chapter 21

The Council's meeting went without a hitch. In the end, to Mumbaza's relief, it was a unanimous vote to go public with the information about Astro. Everyone was anxious but grateful that their first point of action would be to inform the Royal Committee, then the Board of Directors, before they would gain support for a PR campaign to inform citizens. They knew that they would face a lot of questions from all groups, but the relief from all of The Council was palpable.

Sisi, backed by Queen Sia and Queen Silvia, took charge of the meetings with the Royal Committee and then the Board of Directors. The meetings went as well as could be expected, but in the end, the depth of the news took over any sense of anger. Most could not adjust to the news given, as if they had just been told of an impossibility.

The public campaign started just two weeks after the Royal Committee and Board of Directors had found out. Everyone who worked on the campaign agreed that it was impossible to manipulate the information in any way in order to dampen the effect, so they presented just facts to the public. A one-page statement explaining the situation in simple terms was distributed alongside links and access to more in-depth scientific information. It also announced that Blue Planet would be presenting on preparations and steps taken in two weeks' time. Tensions ran high at the Blue Planet Headquarters as all waited in their stations to manage reactions and questions. However, there were only a few calls and messages.

After two weeks, they continued with the second phase of the public campaign. Queen Sia led the presentation of the preparations on Moon and on the development of the Pulse Generating Canon whilst Dr. Benjamin Mitchell presented the anthropological facts on the possibility of a sentient species on board Astro. The Royal Committee and the Board of Directors ensured that the information presented was factual and non-biased, hoping that it would encourage the public to consider all facts neutrally and help with the voting.

All on The Council, including Queen Catherine, felt proud of how the information was shared, forgetting that they had held these secrets for fifteen years. Although she was anxious about the outcome of the public campaigns, Cate felt relieved that there were no longer any secrets—other than Mumbaza's mortality, which served as a reminder to the few conspirators of the origin of the problem.

In the two months since The Council started to inform others about the secret discoveries, there was a public voting held to determine whether the development of the Pulse Generating Canon on Earth would proceed, as a safety measure. The public were told that if humanity were to come under any threat from Astro, this new weapon would be able to remove the threat, protecting all.

"If we believe that The Burrowers exist and that they are sentient, then this would be wrong!" cried Queen Catherine, as she, Mohamed, Mumbaza, Sarah and Qamari waited in Mumbaza's flat for results of the voting.

"We're not voting to use the weapon, Cate, just to build it," suggested Sarah, trying to calm Cate.

"Sarah's right. It is a worst-case scenario thing. Risk management, right?" Prince Mohamed tried, hoping that Mumbaza would agree, too. Mumbaza was already shaking his head alongside Cate.

"Our past has taught us that if we arm ourselves, it would be to cause harm. Never for peace. Peace is only achieved when we do not have weapons. No matter who or what the Burrowers may be."

"But if the Burrowers are aggressive—"

"Then we would have been attacked by now," Mumbaza added, not allowing Mohamed to finish his question. They had mulled over the same ideas again and again in many disguises, amongst different groups, but they all knew deep down that it was up to the votes now.

"Perhaps it doesn't matter, but we have had fifteen years to deal with this knowledge in our own minds, but the public are voting after just two months," Catherine pushed on, hoping that Mohamed, Sarah or Qamari might consider changing their positions. They just sat quietly staring at the vote results being counted on screen.

The readings showed that over 70% of citizens on Earth have voted, with majority saying 'yes'. Votes were also being taken on Moon and Kagami, each vote coming in as a 'no', slowly giving Queen Catherine and Mumbaza some hope. However, Earth's votes overwhelmed in the end, affirming the decision to go ahead with the development of the weapon.

"That's it then," said Mumbaza resignedly.

"Wait... no..." Cate waved a hand at the rest to let her think. "Won't Astro get data on the plans of the Pulse Generating Canons? If they know, there's not much point in building it, right?"

"Sorry, Cate," Mumbaza reached to hold Queen Catherine's hand, "let it go. All the data streams between Astro and Earth, Kagami, and especially Moon have been stopped by our scientists."

Mohamed nodded as he explained further, "The data connections were actually left intact, but all new data, especially sensitive or military data, are kept on different data streams and formats now, We believe Astro would not be able to intercept these new streams and all the readings on the connections so far confirm that they no longer have access to new information."

Queen Catherine paused to think before she declared to the others, "I cannot just sit by and watch humanity try and gain power through destruction and war. This is an unfair fight."

"But, Cate," Mohamed tried to reason still, "there isn't a fight. We're just building the weapon to protect ourselves in case we need to."

"We don't even know if the Burrowers are real, or if there is anything on board the Astro," added Sarah, clearly tired of this argument. All this while, Qamari just sat as she did, quietly staring at everyone, taking in the situation. She was never one to speak up in any situation, only ever in private with Prince Mohamed, and Sarah.

"If we don't think the Burrowers are real, then no one would agree to building the Laser Bomb."

"I think Cate is right," Mumbaza said, unsurprisingly. "But, Cate," he added, turning to speak to her directly, "the people have made their choice. This is what we worked for, what Blue Planet stands for."

Defeated, Queen Catherine slumped into her chair and buried her hands in her face, holding back her emotions. Unwilling to give up, she started thinking of other possibilities in her mind.

I voted no. Maaike too, and so did all our friends on Kagami.

The two months from when we were told about the discovery of Astro were the most exciting on Kagami. We had found out that Henry and Anuar were on Moon as part of the military operations to protect humanity, in case the spacecraft they found turned out to have aliens on board and that they were aggressive.

Maaike and I read all the documents that Blue Planet had released and they were intriguing. Astro itself was a work of art, with its asteroid-like materials on the outer layer, camouflaging it completely in space. As for the internal scans, we discussed this with all our friends and we were not sure if there could be life forms on board or not. Since Astro's technology was out of our understanding, it was very possible for it to have been completely automated. It could have flown itself into our system, locked on to our data streams and just started downloading, perhaps to be studied when Astro returned to its home planet?

Our teachers and guardians were all shocked from the news; no one could seem to believe that we had a spacecraft parked near us that we did not know anything about. I loved it, as it all seemed to make sense. We had learnt in science and philosophy to imagine our origins and use the discoveries of our scientists to support our hypotheses, and we had always concluded that there must be intelligent life forms out in space other than us. It was difficult to imagine otherwise and the discovery of Astro proved it.

Maaike felt the same way. Most of our friends did too. We couldn't understand why out teachers and guardians, those who were older than us, could not seem to accept the fact.

People were angry when we were told that Blue Planet had known about Astro for fifteen years. It seemed against the concept of corporate democracy that Blue Planet Inc. was about. Maaike and I wondered why Blue Planet would still be so anxious to build the Laser Bomb after so many years that Astro had shown no movement, developments, or even interest in us. It seemed then that the Pulse Generating Canon was as a form of protection, of risk management, in case anything were to happen.

We did not see any threat from Astro, which was why we voted 'no'. We did not think that it was necessary to protect ourselves.

chapter 22

Kagami was almost empty when Maaike and I left. We were on the last shuttle, with a few carers and the last group of the toddlers who were going to Blue Planet's headquarters, rather than to families. I felt sad leaving Kagami, but Maaike was excited about going back to Earth. I had never been on Earth and I felt scared.

Iz and Yhi were nearly four years old then. They were chatterers, always curious about everything around them. I was grateful for their continuous stream of questions as it kept my mind off my worries.

I remember how our school had looked that day when we left. As it was a warm summer's day, the foliage around the main building shaded us from the strong sunlight. The buildings that were all made of wood and locally found organic materials blended into the scenery. Only the straight man-made lines gave away the structure.

All the buildings were empty, when we were so used to seeing them with running children. The military had sent a troop in to ensure that there would be no stragglers left behind after us. Maaike and I were quietly hoping that Henry and Anuar would be amongst the troop, but they were not. We had only received news from our teachers, reports that they were both well and were put to work with some new state of the art technology.

The Council gathered for one last time to finalise their plans to disband as the Royal Committee and Board of Directors moved in to take control. This was not something that The Council had wanted, but everyone knew that it was inevitable. The covert group could never have been kept together after the news went public. The Royal Committee had already declared that everyone in The Council would face investigation. A specially selected group would be leading the investigations that would report on the full history of The Council before bringing it to Court for just action. Although no one was reprimanded for the time being, Queen Catherine and Prince Mohamed could not help but feel smug that they would be able to corroborate with the investigators.

"As we all know, all of us on The Council have officially been suspended from our Blue Planet duties, other than to assist with the development of the Pulse Generating Canon and in handing over the military arrangements," Sisi said to the group solemnly.

"I can't say I'm surprised at this outcome, so I am sure that most of you have considered it too."

The nods around the room were slight but perceptible.

"I suggest that we all be as open as possible to the investigation, as it would help our colleagues find a just solution more easily. I have no doubt that they would see our actions as true—with only the good intentions of humanity in mind."

"Are you crazy?" said Queen Silvia, louder than she had intended, her anxiety coming across clearly. "We swore within this group never to speak a word of who we are or what we do, and you're asking us to be *open* with them?"

"I agree with Silvia," Queen Sia said as her first hit the table with a thud, stressing her anger.

"What's the worst they could do to us?" a few others asked simultaneously.

"We've not violated the constitution directly. The Blue Planet constitution allows for *the withholding of information if agreed by those in the know that the information is too sensitive and volatile for public consumption.*" Sia recited the quote that they were all so familiar with.

"Sia," Sisi said, not without a hint of exasperation in his voice. "It also continues to say that *immediate council must be sought under the Pact of Confidentiality from specialists, in order for the information to be made public as soon as possible.*"

"But that was exactly what we did," Sia insisted as a few others nodded in agreement.

"Yes, but we took fifteen years to do it. Some would consider that *not* to be *as soon as possible.*"

"That's just a technicality."

Nodding, King Sisi tried a more diplomatic stance, "Yes, you are right, which is why we should all cooperate with the investigations and give them the facts. It will help them come to a proper decision."

"Clearly we differ in opinion on this matter, Sisi. We should allow the investigation to pan out. Hopefully there will not be too many victims," Sia responded haughtily, closing the topic once and for all.

After a moment of silence that allowed all the members to collect their thoughts, Queen Silvia proceeded with the rest of the final report.

Since the Royal Committee and Board of Directors have taken over on the developments, they have also implemented many changes. The most drastic of which is the mass migration of all citizens back onto Earth. The Pulse Generating Canon would be useless if it does not have a large enough energy source, and it was decided that the most effective solution would be to create more Coughin Centres around Blue Planet's headquarters, where the weapon would be built.

After the approval by the people on the building of the Laser Bomb, all of the parents with children on Kagami were contacted to discuss the future of their children. Many easily agreed that having their children back with their families for a few years would be better than to have them on Kagami, where their futures would be unpredictable anyway. With Astro being situated closer to Kagami, many parents feared that their children would act as sitting ducks out in space.

Blue Planet headquarters was slowly changed into the largest Coughin Centre. Not since the Great War had the population been this small, yet so concentrated in one city so large. All eighty-three floors of the towering glass skyscraper, a monument left from before the Great War during the heydays of capitalism, were slowly morphing into storage floors. They contained nothing but rows and rows of generic Coughin machines, now designed for the usage of anyone who had a chip implant. Some floors homed double-tiered machines that were in bunker-style, whilst others had standing machines facing the glass windows that overlooked the old city.

On every fifth floor, there was a canteen and wash area that stocked all kinds of food and drinks that ranged from healthy to tasty. The popular ones were high-endorphin releasing foods that would cure the lethargy brought on by the lack of movement or exercise, like chocolates and sweets and coffee. The wash area was beautifully maintained by the never-ending supply of help-bots that were cheap to run due to the high output of energy that the Coughin Centres were experiencing. People enjoyed community living in the skyscraper, chatting, laughing, and sharing, without much care in the world. They had minimised possessions down to nearly nothing, depending completely on the facilities provided.

Our shuttle arrived on Earth on a rainy day, but it didn't matter as we exited the shuttle through a covered bridge into the airport. It was overwhelming, seeing the great big block of glass building that was the airport, with many airplanes parked around it. Maaike had warned me about the architecture on Earth, and I had of course seen it in videos and films, but it all felt...unnatural.

From the airport, we were driven to Blue Planet's headquarters as my parents and grandparents were there. Maaike was my family now, so she came with me. I was grateful, as even though I had my father's letters and photographs, I still had no idea what to expect. I was going to meet strangers, really, whose histories I already knew.

Maaike took Iz and Yhi on the journey in the van as they sat up front. She pointed out to various buildings and signage splayed across the top of doorways, explaining how these were historical mementos. Many of the buildings were empty, abandoned after the Great War, but kept open, and anyone could walk in and out of them to be reminded of our cruel past.

Through that journey, I could only stare out into the buildings and billboards that fleeted past in blurs of faded colours and greys. I was grateful that Maaike left me to my own thoughts. We both knew that we would have time to talk about it later, once we had settled down somewhere. At that moment though, we were headed to the main Coughin Centre.

As we approached the building, I was completely overwhelmed by the size of it. My heart had started racing when Maaike lifted Yhi towards me. She smiled, assuring me that everything would be fine. I kept a brave face and calmed my nerves as Yhi excitedly pointed at the building, straining her neck to see the top of it. We were driving into the main entrance, through the basement of the building. It was like the caves that bats lived in, except there were fluorescent lights everywhere and concrete walls in straight lines. As our eyes adjusted to the change of light, Yhi made a little 'woooo' sound on my lap. It made me smile.

We were met at the entrance by Nurse Janice, who was one of the first to leave Kagami for Earth. She had been excited about seeing her children and their families, who were working in various Coughin Centres. She was smiling widely as she greeted us with warm hugs.

We were all given different instructions on where to go. The four of us were to head up to the 61st floor since my family were working there. When we were settled with my family, we would then be registered and prepped for work with Coughin machines.

My family were lounging in a corner, chatting amongst themselves when we arrived on the 61st floor. We followed the floor map given by Nurse Janice and navigated our way through thousands of people. The entire building homed nearly half a million people, all of whom worked and lived at the Coughin centre.

I had held back, unsure about what to say or how to greet them, but Maaike stepped forward and reached out for my mother.

"You must be Magdalena," she greeted her, as my mother stood and both reached their hands out to the other. "You have the same crazy red hair as Sun," Maaike added, bringing smiles all round. "I'm Maaike, Sun's partner, and these are our children, Yhi and Izanagi. We call him Iz."

My father reached out to hug Maaike, then my grandmother did the same. Grandfather was in a Coughin machine not far, looking like he was sleeping very soundly.

After they greeted Iz and Yhi too, father came to me. I remember that his approach was slow and calm.

"Sun?" he whispered, as he was smiling ear to ear. "You're beautiful."

I could only nod as I felt goose pimples at the back of my neck. I stared into his eyes, and they looked just like mine.

He hesitantly reached out one hand to touch mine and when I did not pull back, he held my hand in his, tenderly. I could see my mother and grandmother looking from behind him, each stroking Yhi and Iz's hair lovingly. Maaike looked at me and nodded.

"Dad," I croaked, a sound so odd that it made us all laugh. Even Yhi and Iz laughed along, unaware of the tension.

"Daddy," I whispered again before I broke down crying. He held me in an embrace for a long time before he gently ushered me to my mother. She joined us in a family embrace as she cried too.

We broke from our group hug when we heard Yhi's little voice ask, "Why's mummy crying?" I picked her up and explained that I had never seen my parents before and she nodded like everything made sense. I felt like the child at that moment.

We spent an hour trying to catch-up, though all the questions felt silly and surreal. My parents and grandmother could not imagine life on Kagami, whilst I was having culture shock being on Earth. Maaike seemed to be the only one who had it together that day.

Horace explained to us that we were to report to the floor officer to have our chips implanted, so that we could start work with the Coughin machines. Because the computer chips were programmed with each person's information, it automatically logged the number of hours we would work. We could do so anywhere in the building, or in any of the Coughin Centres nearby too. They showed us the information computers that allowed us to look for empty machines to use. There wasn't any doubt that life at the Coughin Centres was comfortable and somewhat fun, in a social way.

Maaike and I left Iz and Yhi with my family for an hour whilst we explored the building a bit more. We walked hand in hand, which was more for my benefit than hers. We met up with a few classmates who had arrived before us and they were all already working with the Coughin machines. We asked them how the work was, and they all said that it was 'easy', or they shrugged. When we asked them how they spent most days, they seemed to try and get access to the computers in their spare time to read and study. They had missed working on science and research matters.

We returned to my family and found Iz and Yhi sleeping soundly, sharing a Coughin machine as a cot, and we both knew at that moment that we were not going to stay. It must have been obvious, for my father knew it too.

"Are you leaving now?" he asked as I squeezed Maaike's hand for encouragement. I felt her squeeze back.

"Yes. I'm sorry that we're not staying with you and mum and grandma."

"Where will you go?"

"I don't know." We genuinely did not know. "Will Blue Planet stop us from not working here?"

My father shook his head solemnly. "There are too many people in this building for them to track. As long as power levels are high, they are happy." He seemed sad and withdrawn then.

"Then we will walk out and find a place to make our home."

Maaike agreed too as she moved to wake the kids.

My mother's face lit up as she came to stand next to my father. Her voice was soft and sweet, as if she hardly ever used it. "I had heard from others that there is a little abandoned town not far from here. Just follow the road to the west of this building and keep walking away from here. You should come to the town easily." She smiled then, as if she was pleased with being able to help.

"And west is where the sun sets here, right?" I asked and they both nodded.

We said our goodbyes, which were less teary than our hellos. As we walked away from the building, the kids asked us, "Are we going home now?" to which we said, "Yes".

Chapter 23

MAAIKE AND I FOUND the little town that my mother pointed us to. It took us about five hours to walk from the Coughin Centre, nearly three hours to leave the city's boundary. When we came to it, we knew that we would be able to make it our home.

Most of the buildings were abandoned. There were a few buildings with people in them, people like us who did not want to work at the Coughin Centres, people who did not have anywhere to go.

It was nearly dark then, so we approached houses that looked cosy and inviting. The doors were not locked, so we let ourselves in. The houses were fully furnished and decorated as if they were still being lived in, but by spirits or ghosts, perhaps. The second house we went into had two bedrooms; one decorated for children with two smaller beds and the other was the master bedroom. It was beautiful.

There wasn't any power connected to the building, but because it was a warm night we could just open the windows slightly to let some cool air in. Yhi and Iz were very tired, so we gave them some food and water that we had carried with us before putting them to bed. In their sleepy haze, they told us that we were home, and we agreed with them.

After the children went to sleep, Maaike and I checked and explored every corner of the house and we were very happy to find that everything was intact, and clean, albeit a little dusty. We even found some candles and matches and we lit one to keep with us wherever we went. The candlelight was both scary and cosy. I remember feeling exposed, somehow laying my whole self to the world, but I was not afraid, as I knew that with Maaike, we would be safe.

Exhilarated from all the excitement of that day, we decided to mark it by cutting our hair. We both had long ponytails kept in a braid down to our lower backs. It was a uniform for all the girls on Kagami. We found a pair of scissors in the kitchen and without hesitation we cut each other's ponytails.

In the darkness that was lit only by a lone candle, we held both our braids together. My fiery red hair against Maaike's golden blonde, each reflecting different colours from the flickers of the flame. Working in silence, we braided both together into a circle, a garland, and we tied a little notecard to it that said Maaike, Sun, Yhi and Izanagi. Our family and our new home.

From that day onwards, we hung our hair garland on the door of every home we lived in, a sign that it was our home.

That first town that we settled in was called Angel Town. We lived there as a family for nearly two years—the period it took Blue Planet to build the Pulse Generating Canon. In our first month, we explored different parts of Angel Town until we were familiar with all the buildings. We also met the small community of people who were to be our neighbours, our extended family for the two years. At our fullest, there were sixty-three of us in total.

Maaike and I had found the old civic library in our first week and then, we would return every other day to grab a few more books. The house we were in, number eighteen, already had a good stock of books and we were surprised at how well we were able to survive on our own, learning from the books.

We learnt initially that foraging plants would give us vegetable and fruits. We compared notes with books to identify what was edible, and actually, most plants are! We even started planting our own vegetable garden when we found an old shop that had dried seeds. Collecting rainwater, we were able to water the plants consistently. Though some plants only yielded produce after a whole year, there were others that continuously bore us fruits. We gained popularity amongst our small community when we shared our produce and also shared the books that we had found.

It was only two months into our stay when the weather started to get colder. We had read in our books that fireplaces with chimneys used to keep houses warm, but after consulting with everyone we felt that it was too dangerous for us to try building fires indoors, especially since none of the buildings in Angel Town had chimneys or fireplaces.

We collected all the thicker clothing from all the abandoned houses in Angel Town and distributed them by size amongst us. There were many blankets too, but we knew that it would be an uncomfortable winter. None of us had ever experienced true harsh winters before, for central heating was a standard feature in buildings since it came under welfare allowance with Blue Planet. It was a basic need.

Our first autumn came and as the days started getting shorter, our small community found a new member. His name was Orhan and he came bearing gifts.

Most of our neighbours chose houses that were very close to ours, so when Orhan arrived, he could see the cluster of houses that had candles lit, giving out small warm glows.

He had arrived and knocked on Ben and Stacey's door first. Their house was on the next street from ours. They greeted him warmly, but they saw that he was pulling behind him a huge box with two small wheels on it. He seemed tired, but he was friendly. He had asked them if he could stay anywhere and they told him that he could. They suggested that he come to us first, since he might need some food and drink straightaway and we always had a stock in our pantry.

Ben and Stacey brought him over to our place, Ben helping with his huge box and Stacey carrying one of his three backpacks. When everyone had settled in our living room, Maaike took Yhi and Iz up to bed whilst I spooned up the remaining soup that we had left for the day. With the help of our neighbours, we had built an open burner in our garden that we could use to make large pots of food, and we would do this daily.

As Orhan ate, we saw the energy slowly coming back to him. Even when sitting down, you could see that he was tall and lanky. He had tanned skin and a pepper of greys amongst his jet-black hair. He always smiled, even though he was feeling so tired that night.

"Thank you, that was lovely," he said to me as soon as he was done with the last two full bowls of soup.

I cleared the table and Ben helped me make up a pot of peppermint tea. The leaves were grown in our house.

"Where do you get all these supplies?" Orhan had asked us as he held his cup of tea between his palms, warming them.

Stacey answered him. She explained that we learnt about plants through books and we grew them for our own use. "Sun and Maaike found the books at the library and showed us what they learnt from them. We now all read up on different things and share what new things we learnt," she added.

"That's great," he had said, nodding his head vigorously whilst grinning from ear to ear. "You sound like you have a great little community here."

"Yes, we do," Ben, Stacey and I answered simultaneously as we laughed at how silly we sounded. Maaike came to join us again then.

"Can...uhm, can I join your community, please?"

We were shocked that he would even have to ask us and we told him that we would love to have him with us and that we would introduce him to the rest of Angel Town the next morning.

For ease of moving that night, he chose the house next door to us, which we sometimes used for meetings. It was basic and one of the rooms had a large double bed, which suited him well.

Maaike and I helped him settle into his new place that night by giving him some fresh sheets and a jug of drinking water. We also showed him where buckets of water were kept in our garden that he could use to wash. He seemed genuinely happy to be with us and kept thanking us. He didn't seem to mind the lack of comforts our lifestyle demanded.

"If you don't mind, Orhan, can we ask you about why you came here?" Maaike gently prodded as we were about to leave and let him rest.

"No, of course not. I don't agree with the work that Blue Planet assigned for me, and I thought that my best option was to leave altogether. I had heard about Angel Town, so I packed up and walked here."

"What did you do?"

"I...I am, no, I was one of the engineers for the Pulse Generating Canon." That was the only time that night that he looked genuinely sad.

"Oh..." was all we could say in return. We never imagined ever meeting anyone who worked for Blue Planet directly, let alone a Laser Bomb engineer.

"But," he said with a smile again, "I realise that you do not have heating in Angel Town and I believe I can help with that."

"How?"

"Well, for the town, I will need to study the development plans and charts to see how the electric lines are laid out, and I can probably wire a street up with electricity. They should have these in the town hall or civic centre."

I told him that we'd been to the town hall and had seen the offices, so we could probably find them quite easily.

"Great. Good. But for the source of the energy, well, that might be more…sensitive. You see, that there," he had said pointing at the large box that he was lugging with him, "is a Coughin machine."

Maaike and I both stared at the machine. It was covered in a dark coloured tarp, but we could make out the shape very easily now.

"I can use it myself and I would be happy to provide Angel Town with what energy is needed…" he paused there for a long while, before saying, "if it is ok with everyone, of course. I know that most people, if not everyone here in this town came to get away from these machines."

We nodded. "Why don't we discuss this with everyone tomorrow?"

Orhan agreed with us and we bade him good night. It was already quite late in the night.

The next day, we woke early to cook a few pots of porridge. We had found dried oats in an old food store and most of them were still in a good state. Everyone loved a hearty breakfast of oats that we boiled with water and everyone could top it up with a fruit preserve of their choice. It wasn't even nine in the morning when a large crowd had gathered, so we went to ask Orhan if it would be ok for us to continue to do our meeting in his house, since it had the large open kitchen and living room that could accommodate all of us.

He was already awake, probably awoken by the sounds of chattering, and readily agreed as we brought the large pots of porridge over. Everyone knew to bring their own bowls. As we tucked into our breakfast, the children played in the garden and Angel Town got meet its new resident. Everyone took to Orhan immediately, happy for the addition.

We gathered to discuss Orhan's suggestion the night before and we were surprised that many agreed to allow Orhan to provide us with electricity. We had not known before, but there were quite a few others who had worked with Coughin machines before and were willing to help out too.

It was decided that we would continue with all manual labour and that electricity would only be for heating and the use of one computer that would remain in Orhan's home that would allow us to follow news from Blue Planet. It seems the Pulse Generating Canon was nearly halfway done and there were more Coughin Centres built around the main one to help provide and store energy. Bar a scattering of communities like ours dotted outside the city margins, Orhan told us that the data held by Blue Planet's scientists recorded that there were approximately 46.5 million people, now all living on Earth. Over 40 million of those people were in the main city, living and working in one of the many Coughin centres. When we had learnt in school about the problem of humanity's dwindling population, it was still at over 100 million people and the minimum one child policy was going to maintain it at that. It was shocking to hear that the discovery of the spacecraft could have changed Blue Planet's priorities so much.

The day that we had walked from the city to Angel Town, we had seen a few cars on the roads with people transporting goods around. Orhan said that when he walked to Angel Town, it was quiet on the roads; there was not a single person and only a few automated vehicles. Most things were artificially produced by machines, and those machines were installed in every other building in the city. Even foods were mostly chemical inventions, full of taste and the right amount of vitamins and minerals required, but unnatural. That was why he was surprised when he found out that we had our own produce.

Orhan quickly became an invaluable part of our little community. He fixed tools that helped us farm better and he brought music to our little town, digging out old record players and finding music records, creating a little library of tunes, as he called it, at his house. Having electricity at night meant that we could stop using candles too, and within a month of moving into Angel Town, he managed to sort out electricity for all of us. Only a few people had to move houses.

With the minimal electricity usage, it took Orhan and three other volunteers who had chip implants for the Coughin machine an hour a week each to provide more than enough energy for all of us. In fact, when there was more than enough in the storage, Orhan would do the top-ups himself, minimising the time the others had to spend with the machine. We knew that until we could find an alternative source of energy, this set-up was the best we could manage.

Orhan's scientific mind also meant that he would experiment with our methods of farming, cooking and even cleaning; always trying out different ways of improving our lives in Angel Town. We were all very content with our lives then, happy to have found this community that allowed us to bring all our children up in the way that our ancestors had, many, many years ago.

That was until we heard that the Laser Bomb was nearly ready.

Chapter 24

"Three months," Prince Mohamed said, as he paced up and down the large living room that was furnished with simple Scandinavian furniture.

"Yes, three months before the weapon is ready." Mumbaza was sitting on a sofa in the same room, looking out of the glass doors that led to the garden.

They had moved into a large house by the edge of the city after The Council disbanded. Prince Mohamed, Queen Catherine and King Sisi were officially under investigation by Blue Planet, but they had yet to have an interview with anyone. The rest of The Council were placed under house arrest, like they were. Initially Mohamed, Cate and Sisi were surprised that no one had followed-up with them after their move, but they knew that Blue Planet were too busy as they had placed top priority on the building of the Laser Bomb. The question of The Council's actions, whether they were traitorous or not, was put on hold.

Sarah decided to stay with Cate even though they were officially not allowed to be working. Qamari wanted to return to her brother and his family, who were all working at a smaller Coughin Centre. She applied for a position there and was accepted directly. They gave her a chip implant immediately so that she could begin work straightaway. She spoke only once again with Prince Mohamed after her move, and though she was sad, she told him that she was happy to be able to spend some time with her brother's family, especially with his two children who were still too young to work with the Coughin machines. Although Mohamed was distraught that Qamari was no longer with him after nearly twenty years of working together, he never let on.

"Are you anxious, Baz?" Mohamed asked, thinking about how ironic it was that Mumbaza was the only one able to leave the house freely, since the rest were under house arrest.

"What for? The investigations afterwards?"

Mohamed nodded.

"I am so happy to be out and free, it's not an issue for me anymore. I am anxious for all of you, of course, but I know that we have all accepted our positions in what happened. I'm just glad to be with friends."

Sisi and Cate brought out mugs of coffee from the kitchen for everyone, chattering happily about coffee making techniques.

"They're clearly not anxious at all," commented Mumbaza, smiling at the odd situation.

"What technique is there to making instant coffee anyway?" Sarah piped up, now that they were all together. Though no longer an assistant, she still felt uncomfortable joining in on any of the more personal discussions.

"You'll be surprised, Sarah. Cate has this marvelous technique that makes it taste that little bit better," Sisi teased, trying to hold back laughter.

"Yes," Cate was ready to share her secret. "You place one teaspoon of coffee powder, two teaspoons of creamer powder and half a teaspoon of sugar, then you mix it together first before pouring in hot water. Now, the water shouldn't be too hot. You want to let it cool for a bit before using it or else it will spoil the taste!"

Taking the coffee from the two, everyone took a sip and made smacking noises humorously, as they broke into laughter.

"Now, Mohamed. What were you and Baz talking about? Let me guess...the completion of the weapon in three months?" Cate found that Mohamed had been getting more and more agitated as they neared the completion deadline.

"Cate, I was just thanking my lucky stars that you came and had the conversation changed, and now you pull it back?" Although Sarah was serious, she knew that they had to talk about it.

They all settled onto the sofas like old friends reminiscing over the past, but they were discussing The Burrowers instead.

After Kagami was vacated and everyone was moved to Earth, Blue Planet scientists continued monitoring Astro and they found that it was moving. It was travelling really slowly, but the trajectory was clear, it was going closer to Kagami. Most people pondered if it would land on Kagami, but it seemed to have stopped, parking itself just outside Kagami's atmosphere. The news had kicked off wild speculations from the Royal Committee and citizens alike, but the consensus was that The Burrowers were real and on board Astro.

When Astro had moved, scientists tried to gather as much data as they could, trying to pinpoint a propulsion system, a drive or engine. Even with robotic probes scouring the surface of Astro as it moved, there wasn't any evidence of technology that Blue Planet could make sense of. These reports had further encouraged reactions from citizens, with requests for Astro to be destroyed to avoid any risky discoveries later on.

"So, now that all of humanity seems to be working to generate enough energy so that the Laser Bomb can be used, do we have any doubt that it will be used immediately?" asked Mohamed.

"The last official report today stated that scientists were optimistic that they would be able to get a minimum of three pulses from the Coughin Centres and energy storage when the Laser Bomb is complete. They are even hopeful to get up to five pulses." Sarah spent most of her time reading reports and making sense of them for the group, when she was not helping them create a concise and objective report to defend themselves on The Council investigations.

"Why? Do they think they will miss?" Cate joked, but no one laughed.

"We need to do something about it," Mohamed whispered, his voice barely under control.

"Mo," Sisi, who was sitting next to Prince Mohamed turned and tried to calm him with a hand on his shoulder. "It is out of our hands now. It is with the people, with citizens. It's the masses' choice."

"No, actually. I have an idea." Mohamed was calmer, but the rest could sense his determination. They did not dare stop him or contradict him, so they waited for him to continue.

"We can tell The Burrowers. Warn them. If we're going to destroy them, it is only fair to let them know."

"But that would start a war!" Cate exclaimed, shocked that Mohamed had been considering such an extreme idea.

"Is this not already a war?" Mohamed asked in return. "We are planning to destroy their entire spacecraft when they had not even lifted a finger at us, so to speak. Least we could do is to say to them 'Hey, we're scared of you and we don't know what to do, so we're going to blow you to bits'. No?"

The room was silent then, except for the news feed being played on the television in the next room. It was reminding them of the imminent completion of the Laser Bomb.

Sarah broke the silence first. "I agree with Mohamed."

Cate and Mumbaza looked at her, surprised, but Sisi just nodded in agreement.

"It would be quite simple, really. We could just send them an email attaching the blueprints for the Laser Bomb." Sarah explained, as if they were just planning a party.

"I have my issues with humanity, don't get me wrong, but this is going against our own kind," said Queen Catherine in disbelief.

"So, you believe that The Burrowers are really out there? And that they're sentient?" Mohamed asked as he tried to press his point.

"I… yes, I guess I do believe that."

"If they are sentient, then why don't they have the right to live? What gives us the right to attack them?" The other three sat and watched as Mohamed and Catherine went through what they had been talking about since their house arrest, but with more urgency.

"I don't know. I just know that it is wrong to kill our own."

"But am I suggesting that we set the Laser Bomb to point at us? No. I am merely suggesting that we give them a chance to know of what might happen."

"And what if they retaliate? They might have even more powerful weapons."

"And what if they don't? They haven't done anything to us for more than a decade. If they know that they might be under attack soon, they might just leave."

"What if they attacked us before we attack them?"

"If they could, they would have already. Don't you see? We've always been sitting ducks here."

"I…I just…no, I can't justify it. Why should we take action for something that we have been barred from dealing with. We don't have any more responsibility on this issue and all decisions are made by citizens, so let it be on our collective conscience instead. Not on yours, nor mine, nor any single person's."

"Are you saying that the Laser Bomb is wrong?"

"Of course it is. You know I have always been against it!"

"Good. No, I just wanted to be sure… So, do you think that the collective decision to go ahead with the building, the completion and the usage of the Laser Bomb is wrong?"

Catherine considered this question longer than the rest. She could see where the discussion was leading to but she knew she had to persevere to get closure. "Yes, I think what we're doing is wrong."

"If we warned The Burrowers, would you feel that it is the right thing to do then?"

"No, I don't think it is right. But, I can agree that if The Burrowers are sentient, then it would be the moral, or just thing to do." Catherine slumped in her seat, defeated.

"Even if the rest of humanity disagrees?"

Mumbaza stood up and stopped them, saying, "That's enough. You're breaking her," as he moved towards Queen Catherine to comfort her. "I think all of us in this room agree with you, isn't that enough?"

"No, Mumbaza. Don't you see? We are all in turmoil ourselves. I know that it is the right thing to do, but yet, I cannot justify it to myself to do it. Don't you see, we've ruled, governed, led communities, states, even countries in the past. We thought we got it right with the creation of Blue Planet Inc., with the end of the Great War, but we don't! Humanity is just a farce. We make a big weapon and we think we're in control. We can't seem to control or govern our own selves, and yet we want to 'defend' our world from aliens. Aliens that we cannot even try to fathom what they are or where they came from!"

Mohamed slumped into his seat, exhausted from his outburst. The rest stared into their laps, not knowing what to say or do.

Sisi stood up and paced in front of the group, snatching their attention. They could see that he was gathering his thoughts and they waited until he was ready to share.

Sisi stopped in his tracks and looked at his friends around him and he said to them, "Ok. If we cannot know whether our actions are right or wrong, let's do it to bring balance."

He looked around the room and was glad to see that they were nodding to urge him on.

"For all we know, the data stream to Astro might have picked up the military secure connections from us, anyway. But if not, and we are able to send them information on the Laser Bomb plans, then it would just level the playing field, right?"

"That's true," Sarah said as she started to see where Sisi was headed. "We don't know if they are able to understand our text, let alone our science. Giving them the data would just complete the information they have on us, whether they were planning to use it or not."

"Say we agree to do that," said Cate cautiously, "can we actually do it? Do we have access to the open connection between Earth and Astro?"

Caught up by the collective enthusiasm, Sarah made a suggestion. "I have an idea and it could work, I think."

Nodding, everyone encouraged her to go on.

"Once we have prepared the documents and data that we want transmitted, I could bring Baz to the Communications Room. Usually, only the engineers are there monitoring stuff, and they rarely ever get visitors, let alone Royal ones."

"Why me?" asked Mumbaza, curious and excited on the notion of being able to participate actively.

"Well, currently, it's only you and me who are not under house arrest, so we won't attract unnecessary attention. Also, since you've been gone," she said waving her fingers on the word gone, "many probably do not remember what happened. I might be able to get you in on your old credentials."

"Even if you got in," Mohamed asked, playing along with the plan, "would they let you upload the files?"

"Yes," Sisi answered instead. "It's a great idea, Sarah." Turning to the rest, he explained, "Whenever we used to bring documents over to be distributed globally, the engineers would never question them and just do it, as they would have received a message from the Royal Committee beforehand. That could just be an email from anyone on the Royal Committee."

Encouraged by Sisi, Sarah continued, "That email is very easy to fake. They don't ever check them and they just look at the signatory and the email address it's from. So, if we sent an email just before we head there—we can see if Baz's old Royal Committee email address still works—we can tell them that King Mumbaza and I are heading over with an urgent document to be uploaded onto the Astro communications stream. If they question us when we're there, Baz can explain that it is a new military approach used to distract The Burrowers. A sort of protection where if The Burrowers are deciphering our data, this would throw them off our scent, distracting them from the Pulse Generating Canon."

"It sounds…too simple," Cate said as she contemplated the plan.

"Yes, and of course there are many things that can go wrong. For example, they might remember that King Mumbaza is supposed to be dead."

"True, but if we could help," Mohamed suggested, "create a distraction or something, then we might be able to minimise the risk of anyone thinking too hard."

They proceeded with the planning and set a date a month away, giving The Burrowers a two-month warning if they were successful. Glad for the distraction and purpose, they went through their plan step-by-step, prepared for any eventuality and Sarah and Mumbaza resigned themselves to facing Blue Planet judgement should they get caught. They decided that they probably wouldn't be in any worse a situation than they were in already.

Chapter 25

The first number that Orhan wrote on his door was '30', as he followed Blue Planet's countdown to the completion of the Pulse Generating Canon and its usage. He explained to us that we needed to seek shelter when it happened, and remain in shelter for a week at least, to avoid any possible radiation. Blue Planet had already been taking steps to protect the city and with all citizens in Coughin Centres and not outdoors, it was easy for them.

However, Blue Planet would not be protecting anyone outside the city, as they were seen to be defects. Officially, anyone not contributing to the cause for protecting humanity was placed at the lowest priority.

We, the inhabitants of Angel Town started making arrangements to seek shelter in the underground tunnels that the old transportation systems used. There was one in Angel Town that was very deep—deep enough for us to be sure that any radiation would not get down to that level.

We spent most of the month cleaning part of the underground tunnel and bringing blankets and cushions down, to create a more comfortable space. We also gathered as much dried food and clean water as we could get, hoping that it would be enough for more than the week we would spend down there. Then, we tried to spend our days normally, whilst Orhan kept a close eye on the news, waiting for the final countdown.

"Those under house arrest are invited to move into the main Coughin Centre at 0600 hours on Monday, as protection against any possible radiation leakage. This is a courtesy offer by The Royal Committee and is not compulsory. If you would like to take this offer up, you must make your own way to the main Coughin Centre and be there no later than the time set above." Mumbaza read the notice that they had received, just two days before the completion of the Laser Bomb.

"So, should we go?" asked Cate.

"Why not?" Mohamed shrugged.

"What about me?" asked Mumbaza, who was still unsure of how news of him being alive would be received by the rest of the Royal Committee.

Their little operation a month earlier was more successful than any of them had imagined. The engineers at the Communication Centre did not question what was being uploaded, though Mumbaza volunteered the fake information out of anxiousness. Aware of how overwhelmed the engineers were with the presence of a Royal Committee member, Mumbaza even managed to add before they left the centre that the engineers should not speak about the visit to anyone, since it was a matter of national security. Even though Sarah and Mumbaza never for a minute thought that would work, since Blue Planet Inc's constituency is all about open knowledge and open information, they were glad that they had not been tracked down yet.

"You can't hide forever, so why not come with us?" suggested Cate. "Sarah, will you come with us too?"

"I have nowhere to go anyway, so I'll come if Baz comes. Else, I can stay here with him." Sarah tried to sound nonchalant, but they were all aware of the risks involved.

"No, you're all right. I should come with you since it'll be much safer. I'm going to have to face the music soon enough anyway. So, why not now?" Mumbaza decided as they all packed up the little possessions they had, bringing with them only their tablets and a spare change of clothes.

The small team rested well through the night before they had an early start in setting out on their walk to the main Coughin Centre. Since they were at the edge of the city, the walk took nearly three hours.

At the Coughin Centre, they arrived to a building that was calm, quiet and eerie. When they logged onto the reception computer, announcing their arrival, it just displayed a message for them to head to the 24th floor, where they had been allocated a room for the week. There were no additional instructions, other than that they were expected not to leave the building for that period.

They moved slowly up the building, taking time to peep on each floor, but all they saw were Coughin machines in use. There were a few people on each floor who were not plugged in, and were helping monitor usage, but they were few and far between, difficult to spot amongst the thousands of Coughin machines on each floor.

Queen Catherine and Prince Mohamed, who had both used to manage and help out at these Coughin centres were both shocked at how quickly things have changed. The automation of the processes and of the machine production meant that there were nearly as many machines as there were people. With the launch of the Pulse Generating Canon approaching quickly, there was no doubt that Blue Planet would have required all to contribute, to ensure that they maximise the number of pulses achievable for maximum effect.

Cate and Mohamed were just glad that they were not part of this nightmare arrangement. Mumbaza, on the other hand, had only ever seen the one machine—Queen Catherine's. At the sight of the thousands of machines laid out on each floor, he struggled to accept it as reality. As they went past floor after floor of machines, making the lift stop on each level to take in the drastic setup, Mumbaza kept mumbling, "This is not living, how is this living? This is not living." Sarah and Sisi could only try to soothe him by holding his arms on either side as they moved. They had seen more reports and were more prepared for being in the midst of the largest Coughin centre.

The group had found their room on the 24th floor, just a small box of a room, but it was situated next to the washing facilities and vending points for food and drinks. They would at least be comfortable. There were also three Coughin machines in the room, with a small desk and computer point with three chairs. They were expected to work whilst at the centre.

Sarah tried to lighten the situation as she said to Mumbaza, "I guess they weren't expecting the two of us."

They moved around the room to make themselves comfortable as they agreed that they would not want to explore the building any further. They would be content to remain in the room and the vicinity around it for the week, without having to see the thousands of machines that shared the building with them, each with a person tucked inside, sleeping soundly.

chapter 26

It was nighttime on a very cold winter's day when the construction bots completed the final checks and declared that the Pulse Generating Canon was done and ready to be used. There were less than twenty people present to witness this momentous occasion. They were mostly engineers and scientists, with three Royals and three Directors.

It was an historical moment as it was to date the most complex and largest weapon ever made in human history. It was also an historical moment because it was the biggest collective effort ever known in human history. Nearly 99% of humanity lay in Coughin machines at that moment, contributing energy so that five pulses may be made in the 24 hours proceeding, and only nineteen people would be witnessing the event with their own eyes.

As the engineers checked the data that the bots provided, the others provided updates that acted more as a log for the archives than information for anyone reading or listening in, for there were only a few. The five on the 24th floor were part of the few. They sat glued to the tablet that they had connected onto the computer point, displaying a ticker stream of texts, factually documenting every step of the launch.

The countdown to the first pulse came in only minutes after news of the weapon completion. There was a whole minute's warning as the five sat counting sixty seconds backwards, but as it reached one, there was a blackout, and the five could not know whether the pulse was successful or not.

Chapter 27

The five were holding hands in the dark for a few seconds before the emergency lights came on. The only time they had ever experienced this was during emergency drills, but that was staged. Still holding hands, they weren't sure what they should do.

In the dull blue lights, bright enough for them to be able to make out large objects and the path to the door, Sisi was the first to speak up and to break the hand-bond.

"Do you think the Laser Bomb worked?"

Mohamed got up from his chair and stretched, asking, "Do you think The Burrowers stopped it?"

"Let's investigate," suggested Sarah, already walking towards the door.

Their eyes soon got used to the dull lighting and they could move around confidently, although they were scared. As they manoeuvred through the pantry area, they noted that all the vending machines were switched off. The only thing electrical switched on were the dull blue emergency lights that were probably running on a small generator in the building.

As they arrived at a section of Coughin machines, they froze in their steps, each taking time to get used to what they were saw. Rows and rows of people in glass boxes that were reflecting the light blue tint—none of the machines switched on. There was no movement.

Mohamed ran to the nearest Coughin machine and reached in to feel for a pulse. It was faint, but it was there.

"He's alive."

"Can we take him out?" asked Cate as Mumbaza and Sisi stepped around the machine, reaching in, ready to pull the man out on Mohamed's say so.

"I don't know what would happen to him if we just unplugged him." Mohamed turned to look around the room, a gesture that triggered the others to do the same as they took in the gravity of the situation.

"We need to try," said Cate, taking charge.

Nodding, the three men grabbed the man in the machine and pulled him out of the jelly-like material. He felt warm, but lifeless.

"Ok. I am going to unplug his connection," Mohamed said as he carefully reached behind the man's neck, gently holding the adaptor between his thumb and index as he had done so many times before for Catherine. He gently pulled the cable out of the adaptor and nodded to Mumbaza and Sisi to take the man out of the machine completely and lay him on the floor.

They stood around the man staring, waiting for a reaction. He did not move, and after a few minutes, Mohamed reached to check for a pulse. When he felt nothing, he leaned over the man to listen for a breath; any sign of life, but there was none. He looked up and shook his head.

Sarah reached down to the man and gently checked his body for his identification card. Finding one hung around his neck, she lifted it and announced to the group, "His name is Walter Flynn," as she put it back where she had found it.

Cate touched her own forehead, chest, then shoulders, mimicking the sign of a cross, a gesture that was rarely seen anymore and she whispered, "May you rest in peace Walter Flynn".

"Amin," said Mohamed, as Mumbaza echoed with "Amen".

Standing, Sarah and Sisi both looked around the room again.

"There must be someone around. Let's try and gather those who were monitoring the machines," Sarah said, breaking the spell of misery.

"You're right," Cate said as she stood up. "We need to gather our wits and think straight."

"Sisi," Mumbaza called. "Why don't you and Sarah try and see if any of the communications devices work. We need to try and find out what had happened and try to get help."

"Yes, and the three of us will gather anyone who is not in a machine. We'll split up and do just this floor and meet back at the room."

When they gathered back at their room, it was after two hours and they had found only two people, both of whom were engineers with basic medical training, who were stationed to keep an eye on the machines. Even though they were both in shock, Cate managed to glean from them that there were only two people on every floor, monitoring the machines. No more.

Sisi and Sarah were having no luck with their task. None of the electronic devices were working, not even the portable ones. It was as if someone had shut down all modern technologies with that blackout.

They all looked outside of the tall glass windows and saw the sun coming up for a new day. Even though they were all tired, they persevered and Mohamed, Cate and Mumbaza continued with their search for others, on other floors. Sisi and Sarah continued trying to find different methods of communications.

They passed a week with little rest, and an addition of twenty more people to their group. They moved everyone to the tenth floor where there were canned food and bottled drinks that they could survive on. Some of the other engineers who were on monitoring duty tried to unplug some people from the machines, and they had the same outcome. People were getting fearful as the death toll was rising and they feared that the rest of the Coughin Centres out there were the same.

Chapter 28

We couldn't receive any news from Blue Planet as soon as we were all underground. We decided to remain underground for a week, as that would be enough time for any residual radioactivity to pass, before we would head back up. The children found it exciting as we made it an exploration trip. They didn't want to go up with us in the end, asking if we could do it again.

When we went back to our homes in Angel Town, we found that nothing had changed. All our food, water, and plants were as we had left them. There was no sign of radioactivity. We all took time to clean up and settle back into our homes before we gathered at Orhan's house to get some news, but he had none. It seems that whatever had happened took out our only news connection with Blue Planet and our electricity connections too. We were back to having no heating, which we were able to cope with.

Maaike and I felt uncomfortable, knowing that something had happened, but yet we didn't know what. That night, we decided that we would bring Iz and Yhi for a walk into the city. We at least wanted to know that our family was safe at the Coughin Centre.

We told the others of the plan and they agreed, some giving us names of their relatives so that we may find out about them too. Orhan couldn't fix us a connection with our tablets, so he went to an old shop and found a couple of old wind-up radios. Studying the old books, he managed to rig them up to work as two-way radios. He showed us how to use it and we agreed that we would check in as often as we could. We packed enough dried food to last us three days at the most as we did not intend to stay longer.

Chapter 29

Our walk to the city was the same route as we had taken leaving it before. Nothing had changed much, with most of the streets still empty. When we entered the city and neared the Coughin centres, we knew that something was not right as we could see a few people on the streets, looking lost.

We approached a small group of three people huddled together in front of a building and they seemed to have been crying. They told us that nothing works inside of the buildings and that people were dying in the Coughin machines. They didn't know where any of the Royals or Directors were. That small group roamed the streets around their building just to speak to others, but they go back in for food and shelter.

We told them that we came from Angel Town, where there was a good supply of food and comforts, if they wanted to go there. We also told them that we were headed towards the main Coughin Centre first, to look for anymore survivors. They could not face seeing more Coughin machines with bodies in them, and so, they decided to walk to Angel Town. We asked for their names and radioed back to Orhan so that they could prepare for new arrivals. We warned them that there would be more as the city was in a state of despair.

It was difficult for us to describe the scene to Orhan, so we told him that things were very bleak, and that we couldn't be sure of how many people survived the blackout while still plugged into the Coughin machines. We knew that we had to prepare for the worst, even if the worst seemed to be inconceivable.

Cate was leading two people whom she had found on the 26th floor down towards the tenth floor where they had set-up a base near the food store. They knew that they should leave the building to search for help or other survivors, but they couldn't leave all those who were in the Coughin machines.

As they arrived on the tenth floor, Cate was greeted by Sisi and Mumbaza who had been taking in stragglers from the streets who had abandoned their own buildings. They had with them two women, each holding hands with a boy and a girl, all of whom looked healthy, somewhat unnaturally. Cate realised that it had been a long time since she had seen anyone who was not tired or miserable and she found these two women off-putting.

"Cate, meet Sun, Maaike, Izanagi and Yhi," Sisi introduced them. "We found them at the lobby, looking to find their relatives." Turning to the four unlikely visitors, he said, "This is Queen Catherine."

"Please, just call me Cate. Where did you come from?"

"We were living in Angel Town, which is about five hours from here. We came as we couldn't get any news from Blue Planet and we knew about the Laser Bomb. We just wanted to check that our family is ok," said the redhead.

Although Cate had many questions, including where Angel Town was, she only managed to say, "You're very familiar…" as she tried to think of where she might have met Sun before.

Caught off guard by the question, which seemed odd under the circumstances, Sun replied, "Oh, I don't think we would have met before. Maaike and I are from Kagami. I grew up on Kagami from when I was a baby until two years ago when the news of Astro broke."

Nodding, they led their new visitors from the stairwell onto the tenth floor, where they introduced them to the rest.

As Sarah explained the situation to Sun and Maaike, Cate found some paper and pen, and taught Yhi and Iz to play games that she had played as a child. They played Tic-Tac-Toe, they folded origami and they even played the word guessing game, hangman. It was a relief for Cate to have the two children distracting her from the situation, from reality. She had not realised how tired she was until then.

Mohamed managed to check some of the higher floors and had returned with two more new people when Maaike and Sun radioed back to Orhan to give them another update. They confirmed that because of the blackout, most people were stuck in the Coughin machines, and that they could not be removed without hurting them. Maaike also suggested to Orhan that he warn the others to ready themselves for more new arrivals. They could see that many of the survivors were not coping well with the situation and would benefit from their community's help.

After the radio call, Sun and Maaike showed the old radio system to Sarah, Sisi, and two other engineers who were there. They explained how it worked. The others were happy to have found a communication tool that worked and started to search the stores in the building for old computer parts that they might be able to put together to use as the same. In the meantime, Sun left their radio with Sarah, telling her to maintain hourly reports with Orhan, so that they may track those who have started on their way to Angel Town.

Sun and Maaike wanted to still go and see Sun's family, even though they knew that they would not be in any different a situation from the others. When they told the others about it, Mohamed was the first to make the connection.

"Are you Howard and Magdalena's daughter?"

Shocked at hearing her parents' name spoken, Sun nodded and reached for Maaike's hand.

"I'm sorry to be so direct, but you do look just like your mother. Cate and I were on Moon when your parents were there, with your grandparents too."

Cate stopped playing with the children and turned to look at Sun, and she gasped at the resemblance. Sun's hair was shorter than her mother's when they had met her, but it was the same fiery red. She was as beautiful as her mother, but with her father's green eyes, adding to her mysteriousness.

Cate stood up and walked towards Sun, with tears in her eyes.

"Sun, I'm so glad to see that you and Maaike have such a lovely family. I am so sorry about your parents and grandparents."

"It's not your fault, Cate. It's nobody's fault. They were just doing what everyone else did," Sun said as she gestured around them.

With a new burst of energy, Cate grabbed Sun's hand and pulled her to the door as she asked aloud to the room, "Does anyone know which floor Horace and Magdalena are on?"

"They were working on the 61st floor when we visited them two years ago, so they should probably still be there," suggested Maaike as she collected Iz and Yhi to follow them out.

"In that case, let's walk up to the 61st floor with you. We might be able to find others there too."

Chapter 30

SARAH REMAINED ON THE tenth floor to continue work with the engineers to try and build a radio. Cate, Mohamed, Mumbaza and Sisi led Maaike, Sun, Yhi and Iz, as the large group slowly made their way up to the 61st floor. Everyone was surprised at how calm the children were. They seemed to be content with just each other's company, occasionally turning to an adult with a question, which was always met by a truthful and plain answer.

They stopped on every tenth floor to give their legs a break from the upward climb. On their first stop, they came to a floor that was just a complete open floor with no rooms, and just rows and rows of Coughin machines in double bunks. Mohamed told them that he had searched this floor the day before and had not found anyone.

They walked through the machines to a small communal area with chairs so that a few of them could sit for a while. But as they weaved through Coughin machines, Yhi and Iz stopped chatting between themselves and turned to their mothers.

"Mummy, what is that?" Yhi asked Sun as she pointed at the head of one of the Coughin machines near them.

"You know what a Coughin machine is, dear."

"Yes, but that, inside. Look," Yhi said as she pointed near the head of the person in the machine. There was a blue tint coming from the cable that connected the machine and the person.

"I see it," said Sisi, leaning in to have a closer look.

The cable seemed to give out a soft blue glow and on closer inspection, they had found that the entire cable was the same. When they reached to touch any of the cables around them, they were all shocked to find that the cables felt like plant stems rather than rubber insulation that they were expecting. Checking their fingers, the colour did not come off, nor did it leave any smell.

"I don't know, Yhi. I don't think we have ever seen anything like this before," Sun answered, stating what everyone was thinking.

"Let's trace the cable to the source, maybe we can find something there," suggested Maaike as they crouched to their knees to follow the cables from the machines.

The cables ran below the floorboards, which they could easily pry and lift off to follow its trail. As they got closer to the power source, where most of the cables in that section were connected from, they could see that the cables were a stronger, brighter shade of blue, some even giving off a pulse.

Where cables were intertwined, they merged together like a thicker bark, but still malleable. And where there were sockets and adaptors, there were just large bulbous shapes in purple that resembled a fruit or a potato. The bulbs were rough to feel, but clean.

"Mummy, is this a new plant?" Iz asked as all six adults were quietly absorbed in trying to make sense of what was happening.

"I don't know, dear. Maybe…" Maaike said as she and Sun traced the cables back to the Coughin machines.

"It has affected all the cables that run into every machine on this floor," Sun said as they returned to huddle as a group.

Mohamed took a cable in both hands and tried to pull it apart, but it did not give. The pulsation got brighter when he applied pressure, as if it was a warning.

"Mo, perhaps you shouldn't do that," Cate suggested, prying his hands away from the cable as they continued staring.

"I think it's alive!" Sun exclaimed, as if she had an epiphany.

As Sun and Maaike looked at each other, Maaike knew then what had to be done. "Is there an empty Coughin machine here?"

"There are on the 25th floor. Our room, there are three there, why?" Mumbaza said as he led the group towards the stairwell, sensing the urgency in Sun and Maaike's actions.

"We're not sure yet, but we'll know when we see the machines."

The climb up the next five floors was quick and quiet. Mumbaza led them with a purpose and everyone followed urgently, even the children.

They arrived at the room that they were allocated just a week ago to find that all three Coughin machines were still there, but glowing blue. Whatever it was had spread throughout the machines, taking over every electronic part of it and turning it into blue and purple plant-like parts.

In the room, Sun dropped to her knees to face the two children and told them, "Mummy needs to go into that machine, ok?"

They nodded at her, as if they understood why she had to do it.

Maaike took the children and hugged them close as she leaned in to give Sun a lingering kiss. Maaike whispered into Sun's ear as they parted and they both smiled.

"Are you really going into one of the machines?" asked Cate, unsure if it was a good idea.

"Yes."

"But you don't have the chip implant, the adaptor," Mohamed pointed out.

"It doesn't matter," Sun said as she stripped to her underwear and then climbed into the nearest machine.

The rest looked on as she sunk into the jelly, and the blue cables came to life and adjusted themselves around her neck and limbs. Within minutes, Sun looked as if she had been in the machine for a long time, with all the cables growing around her.

She turned her head to look at Maaike and smiled confidently before she closed her eyes and fell asleep.

chapter 31

THE MOMENT SHE WAS connected to the machine, Sun knew that she was not alone and that she was entering a different mind-space. Somehow, she realised that she was in The Burrowers's arena, the species on Astro. She wasn't scared though, even though it felt like she was falling into darkness, as if she was travelling through pure space that provided no comfort, not even a single star.

Sun felt lost in the pitch black for a long time. Long enough for her to think that she was lost forever, but yet, she felt no fear. When she stopped considering where she was and stopped trying to logically understand her surroundings, that was when Sun felt the warmth of light and heard the voices.

They told her that this was an instant of time in her world, that her friends would have only experienced a few seconds since she joined their thoughts. She understood and yet did not know how or why. They then told her to stop questioning and just allow her thoughts to be free and they will be able to guide her and show her what she wants to know.

She trusted them and blanked out her mind, and in an instant she felt them communicate with her. It was nothing like she had ever experienced. The information came in wafts, like waves breaking against her. Between each crash of knowledge, Sun was somehow able to file the new thoughts away into the corners of her mind, defragmenting them into droplets that were tidied away.

She understood then, how everything came to be. She also knew who they were and that there were more sentient species in space watching humanity grow and learn, whilst keeping a distance.

They were many but their thoughts were one, like an intelligent computer with many individual parts. With our words, they may be described as a hive mind, but that would still leave many of their characteristics unspoken. They are old to us, but they are not subjects of time, traversing dimensions as they please. And they act as what we might call space police. Though there are many watching over systems and planets, the Unanimous, as they call themselves in our language, are the only ones who make contact, for they are the most...natural. A difficult concept to translate across thoughts, Sun understood that it meant that they were peaceful and non-disruptive. With the ability to manipulate most elements into an organic state, they acted as doctors to sick planets, but only ever stepped in when necessary.

Sun emerged from the Coughin machine with tears in her eyes. She reached out to Maaike, as if for support, but more intimately for a connection. Her mind worked tirelessly to try and make sense of what had just happened.

"They're all alive, Maaike," Sun whispered, not daring to say anymore in case the act of speaking betrayed more tears.

Maaike pulled Sun close to her body as their children looked on. The rest stood around them, befuddled but yet unable to bring themselves to break that emotional moment.

Sun, with her head buried in Maaike's shoulder, sobbed freely now as her shoulders heaved. Maaike could only sooth her with her presence, not knowing then that it was the best thing for Sun. It wasn't long before Iz and Yhi joined in the embrace, consoling their mother in something that they may never understand.

After what seemed like moments in standstill, Sun broke away from her family and faced the others with a renewed confidence.

"Everyone who is linked up to a Coughin machine is not dead."

"How do you know?" asked Mohamed, who felt the guilt of pulling Walter Flynn out of the Coughin machine, killing him, building within.

"It's the Burrowers. The blue plants are part of them, part of the Burrowers who are on Astro. With our words, they call themselves the Unanimous. It is difficult to explain, but they are many and one at the same time, and they have saved those who were in the machines by welcoming their consciousness into their own," Sun explained calmly.

"What do you mean?" Maaike asked gently. "How do you know this?"

Still holding Maaike's hand, Sun looked at Iz and Yhi tenderly before answering, "They allowed me into their thoughts for what seemed like an eternity, and I slowly gained insight into all that had happened. They only allowed as much information to flow into my mind as I could cope with, any more and I would have lost myself in them. They are a sentient species from a not so distant system and there are many others out there, all observing us, waiting for us to achieve a level of knowledge that would justify them communicating with us." Clearly tired, Sun stopped and closed her eyes, taking time to collect her thoughts.

"You need rest. Should we head back to Angel Town? We can make sense of what you have experienced there, amongst more friends," Maaike suggested.

Sun nodded, allowing Maaike to help her out of the machine and help her get dressed.

"I'm sorry, Sun. I know you're tired, but we need to know a bit more," said Cate, who seemed to be the most agitated by the whole experience. Mohamed, Mumbaza and Sisi looked confused and unable to process what had just happened.

Sun nodded at Cate, encouraging her to ask the questions she had in mind.

"The Burrowers…the Unanimous… if they were real, as you said," Cate paused then, shaking her head incredulously. "Do you trust them? Are they good?"

With a deep breath, Sun replied, "Yes. The Unanimous never caused any harm to humanity, or to any of our homes on Earth, Kagami or Moon. The plan to attack was completely fabricated by us, by Blue Planet. When they knew that we were unable to overcome our primal instincts to fight, abandoning Kagami on a mission to complete a weapon, they knew that we were going to take aggressive action against them. They introduced their technology," she explained as she pointed to the blue cabling across the room, "into our system as we were going to launch our biggest weapon, a weapon that would have not only wiped them out, but also made our world unbearable for us to live in."

Maaike took out dried fruits and shared them out with everyone, passing a bottle of water to Sun too. Glad for the distraction, everyone took a piece of dried apple, savouring every bite.

"It has been so long since we've tasted real fruits," Mohamed commented.

"You should come live in Angel Town, we have natural fruits and vegetables for everyone," Yhi said to Mohamed, bringing a smile to everyone's faces.

When Sun was feeling more energised, she told the group that she would still like to go up to the 61st floor.

"I know you said that they are not dead in the machines, but are you able to bring them out of the machines without killing them?" asked Mohamed, the feeling of guilt returning again.

"It is actually up to the person in the machine. The blue cables are not actually part of the physical beings of the Unanimous. It's their technology—one that is organic, natural. The blue cables provide sustenance for each person to survive in that hibernated state whilst connecting them directly with the Unanimous' mind. Each person in a Coughin machine is part of the hive-mind, though it's a limited access, catered for what the human mind can take. From what I can understand, it is just a hive of human minds that are linked up."

"Was that what you saw?"

"No, I was connected to the main hive-mind, only for a short moment, so that I could understand what was going on."

"When you say that it is up to the person in the machine, why was it that when I took someone out of a machine, he died in my arms?" Mohamed could not hide his emotions any longer as he started to shake in guilt and grief.

Sun walked over to Mohamed and put an arm around him. "It's ok, Mohamed. He didn't die. His mind, his consciousness is now permanently with the collective. When you took him out of the machine, he had a moment to decide if he wanted to remain with the collective or return to his body, as an individual."

They started making their way to the stairs, but this time, they did not stop. They headed as a group directly to the 61st floor. Sun and Maaike remembered where their family was the last time they visited, so they moved directly there.

Sun found her father's machine next to her mother's, whilst Maaike went a little further and found her grandparents' machines side-by-side.

Sun leant over her father's machine so that she was facing him directly as she spoke. "Daddy, it's Sun."

There was a flicker of movement in his eyes.

"I know that you're with the collective, it is ok. I just wanted to let you know that I've come to the Coughin Centre."

There was more movement in his eyes, imitating the REM stage in sleep.

"Would you like to come back, or are you happier with the collective?"

Sun could see a tear forming at the corner of her father's eye as he whispered, "Happy," and smiled.

"Are you with mummy?"

"Yes," he said as Sun looked over to her mother's machine. Magdalena had a sad smile on her face too.

"And grandma and grandpa?"

"Yes."

Sun looked at Maaike who was looking into Mr. and Mrs. Frank's machines. Maaike looked up at Sun and nodded, tears streaming down her face.

"Would you all prefer to be permanently with the collective?"

"Yes. Grandpa is healthy," Horace whispered, as if he was sleep-talking.

"Ok. I love you, Daddy. Mummy too. Be free." Sun smiled, and without hesitation, she reached in and unplugged her father's cable from the adaptor on the back of his neck. She moved to do the same for her mother as Maaike did the same for her grandparents.

Both Maaike and Sun moved towards each other for a long hug, before pulling Iz and Yhi in too. As they broke their hug, Sun spoke with Iz and Yhi, asking them if they knew what had just happened.

They both nodded and said, "They're free."

"That's right. Their minds are with the collective now and they are free of their bodies."

Collecting themselves, Sun and Maaike looked to the others who were just staring on with tears in their eyes.

"You really believe that they are free now, don't you?" asked Cate.

"Of course, or we wouldn't have done that."

"I guess we should start making plans to do the same for everyone," suggested Mumbaza.

"Where is the collective mind? Is it stored somewhere?" Cate asked, needing a more concrete answer.

"I don't know, Cate. All I know is that I was part of it for a moment, and it was beautiful."

They walked as a group down to the tenth floor, joining up with Sarah and the engineers. Sisi ran ahead so that he could brief everyone about what had happened.

When the group arrived, Sarah and Sisi were speaking with Orhan, giving him an update of the situation. There were already eleven new people in Angel Town since Sun and Maaike's arrival in the city.

Everyone looked to Sun for guidance, for answers, but she was too tired and her mind too saturated with information to provide any. Maaike took charge and suggested that they all try and have some food and get some sleep. It would at least be the first night that they would be able to rest well knowing that those in the Coughin machines were ok and that there would be a lot to be done in the next days.

Maaike found a small clean room that was mostly bare for the four of them to spend the night, and as the children slept, Sun and Maaike talked. As they laid on their backs in the foreign room listening to the sleeping breaths of their children,

Sun told Maaike all about her experience with the Unanimous, as one mind. She knew that she would slowly forget most of the experience, as the human brain just is not built for such capacities of thought, so she told Maaike everything.

epilogue

Sun and Maaike led a team, who were known later by historians as 'The Awakeners' through all the Coughin centres. People said that they spoke to the dead in machines and gave them a choice to live again or be free. Those who came back to live would usually be withdrawn for the first few weeks, but slowly, they would forget the Collective and live a fulfilling life. More than half chose to be free in the Collective, leaving not many on Earth.

The Burrowers, or The Unanimous as they would correctly be known later, spoke only to Sun and Maaike. They taught them new technologies that allowed for Earth to be rebuilt, guiding humans to using more natural sciences to help with maintaining a healthy population in a natural habitat.

Though humanity's numbers were low, the developments in natural sciences and the joys in communal living created new open relationships that encouraged new births. The abundance of natural resources meant that pockets of communities could be found across Earth again, all in comfortable lush areas. The old ways of farming were learnt and then taught to newer generations.

When Izanagi and Yhi turned sixteen, The Unanimous made a trip to Earth—the only time they ever did so—to visit Sun and Maaike. That day was the day that people remembered to be the most important in history. It was also the saddest day for Sun and Maaike.

On that day, The Unanimous took Izanagi and Yhi away

with them, together with fifty other children of various ages. They were to be returned to Kagami, their rightful home, where they would lead humanity in a second chance, in rebuilding a new world on a planet that was rightfully theirs.

On that day, The Unanimous also vowed never to return to Earth again, staying close to Kagami only to see the foundations of humanity flourish with the new members. They imparted further knowledge to Sun and Maaike, trusting them to lead humanity on Earth into a new era of peace and fulfilment, entrusting them to be the Queens of Earth.

about the author

Yen Ooi started writing as an outlet for her wild imagination, which was instigated at a young age by her appetite for books. Having had a vibrant career in music touring, education, and project management, in 2008 Yen put her skills towards writing stories — producing speculative, fantasy, and science fiction in various guises. She shares her short stories, poetry, and blog on her website, yenooi.com and is featured in various anthologies. Yen is a BSFA member, and a member and panelist of Worldcon. She shares her home and writing lair in London with her patient husband and two mischievous cats.

Lightning Source UK Ltd.
Milton Keynes UK
UKOW04f0149021214

242503UK00002B/34/P